WIFE

BETROTHED #1

PENELOPE SKY

Hartwick Publishing

Wife

Copyright © 2019 by Penelope Sky

CONTENTS

PROLOGUE

Marrakech, Morocco

THE BAZAAR WAS ON FIRE.

Black cobras hissed at their masters when they heard the sound of the whip, men bravely shoved blades down their throats for entertainment, and gypsies danced for coins. When your donation wasn't generous enough, they slunk behind you and picked your pockets—taking what they deserved.

It was one hell of a place to celebrate my twenty-first birthday.

Damien walked beside me, a cigar resting between his lips. When a group of pretty girls passed, he gave them mere seconds of his attention before he moved on to the next sight. Now he stared at a camel being led away by its master. "What should we do now? Get a rug and take it home?"

"Rugs are nice." I liked Morocco because of the chaos. This city was unpredictable, from the dangerous route to the Atlas Mountains and the constant bomb checks under vehicles anytime you drove onto public property. It was a different kind of place, beautiful but unsteady.

"I'd rather spend my money on pussy—but not take it with me."

The brothels here were exciting—and dirt cheap. "Later." We'd spent the afternoon drinking, smoking, and exploring everything this city had to offer. It was a short flight away from Florence and an extreme change of scenery.

Damien sighed in dismay at my response. Of all the things he loved in life, pussy was his favorite. Booze and cigars were in a close tie for second. But something changed his demeanor when he turned his head and examined the bright purple tent behind the vase stand. "Fortune-teller... that's interesting."

"Is it?" The practice was nonsense, just a way to take your money then laugh at you on your way out.

"I've never done it before. Let's check it out." Damien puffed one last time before he threw his cigar onto the ground and stomped on it. The ashes squished under his shoe, adding to the other filth on the ground.

"You've got to be kidding me."

"What's the harm? We've got nothing else to do for the next few hours."

"Only gypsies read fortunes. She'll learn about us then sell our information to someone so they can rob us."

Damien rolled his eyes. "You think anyone could cross us and get away with it? Come on."

Since I didn't have a better plan for what to do next, I followed Damien inside the mysterious tent. Once the flap closed behind us, we were surrounded by dim lighting, the various lamps around the room giving off different colors of life. The woman sitting at the table was covered in jewels. A blue eye was one of the largest pendants that hung down from her neck. Jewels were also braided into her hair, and the rest of her brown locks were tucked underneath the shawl tied around her chin.

The woman had an array of cards in front of her, and she continued to rearrange them as if we weren't there at all.

Damien approached the table, welcoming himself into the room like he owned it. "You want to read my fortune?"

She kept working the cards, her eyes down.

Damien stared at her, becoming increasingly annoyed by her rejection.

I noticed a table in the corner where at least a hundred candles were burning, their smells combining to form a scent filled with so much cacophony, I couldn't even describe it. There were small vases on the ground, gold-plated with turquoise stones decorating the sides. There were several of them, all the same but, at the same time, all unique. It was the first time I'd ever seen vases in that style.

Damien eventually lost his patience. "I guess you aren't getting paid today." He turned around to look at me. "Come on. Let's get the hell out of here."

"Wait." The middle-aged gypsy stopped playing with her cards.

Damien grinned at me, both of his dimples showing, along with his boyish charm. He turned around slowly, his arrogance rising like the scent from the candles. "That changed your tune quickly."

She kept the same stony face, looking at Damien without blinking once. "I was studying your auras, which are quite different. They say you don't need to speak to a man to know him. All you need to do is feel him. Now, sit." She grabbed her cards and put them into a single deck. "What's your name?"

Damien sat in the old wooden chair. "Aren't you supposed to know that?"

"No. I'm supposed to read your future. In order to do that, I need some information from you."

"My aura wasn't enough?" he asked like a smartass.

She continued to shuffle the cards as she held his gaze. "Your aura is pungent." She pushed a dish toward him. "Your payment."

"How much?" He pulled the coins out of his pocket.

"Whatever you think is fair."

Damien raised an eyebrow before tossing three coins into the jar. "Never heard that before."

The gypsy grabbed the deck of cards and then placed them on the table, organizing them into two rows. She slowly took away cards that seemed out of place until only two were left. "Give me your palm."

He rested it on the table.

She grabbed his wrist, felt around for a few seconds, and then studied the lines in his palm. "Would you like to know your future?"

"Why else would I be here?"

She continued to ignore his rough attitude, and her only response was to give him a cold look with her brown eyes. "The future is a scary thing. Knowing what will befall you is considered a curse more than a blessing."

"I'm not asking how I'm going to die. I was expecting a fortune cookie-type of thing."

She raised an eyebrow. "Then maybe you should have eaten Chinese for lunch. This is a true reading. I've had many people return to me in anger because this conversation ruined their lives."

"Right..."

I lingered in the corner, listening to their conversation as I observed the contents of the small tent. It was warm inside because there was no airflow, and it was a hot summer night. But everything she had as decoration was so thick and heavy. The rugs on the floor retained the heat of the room, and the fabric of the tent itself was so thick, none of the outside light could penetrate the material.

The gypsy looked into his palm once more. "Alright. You will be a rich man. Very rich."

His shoulders stiffened immediately. "Good to know."

"You will have more money than you could ever spend in one lifetime."

"Even better..."

"But you will be alone. And you will lose many people you love on the way. One woman will love you for you, not your money or your power, but you'll lose her. And once she's gone...she's gone. Your life will be filled with regret, mistakes that can never be undone."

Damn.

Damien kept his cool. "Well...at least I'll be rich." He rose from the seat and clapped me on the shoulder. "Good luck, buddy."

I didn't care about learning my fortune, even if it was a bunch of bullshit. But I dropped into the chair anyway. My knees were planted far apart, and my hands rested in my lap because I wasn't eager for a strange woman to touch me.

The gypsy didn't look at Damien when she addressed him. "Leave us."

"What?" Damien asked. "He heard my fortune. He doesn't care if I hear his."

"Leave us," she repeated, with more tension.

Instead of challenging her, Damien stepped out of the tent and swore under his breath.

When it was just the two of us, it became quiet, the tension slowly rising as our eyes remained locked. The sounds of the surrounding crowd were still audible, but it was muffled by the thick tent that insulated us.

With just her expression, she showed far more interest in me than she had with Damien. Then she took the bowl with the money away.

I watched her movements then raised an eyebrow. "You will not read my fortune?"

"Yes. But I won't take your money."

That was the first time I'd ever heard a gypsy say that. "I don't know if I should be concerned or flattered."

"Very concerned. It's not often someone steps inside my tent and disrupts all the energy in the room. Your presence is profound, scary. Your future terrifies me."

This was one hell of an act. "If you think you're going to pick my pockets, not gonna happen." I had eyes in the back of my fucking head. If someone tried to stick their hand down my pants, they'd get a punch to the jaw.

She shuffled the cards then dispersed them onto the table. "I don't want your money. It's tainted."

"Tainted how?"

"Because of the way you earned it. It's blood money."

My eyes narrowed because she wasn't wrong.

She moved the cards around until she was only left with three. She examined each one. "Fire. Demon. Death."

I glanced at the cards then looked at her once more. "You picked those cards."

"No. They picked me." She grabbed my wrist and started to touch my skin. She examined my palm, a concentrated expression on her face. "All your ambitions will come true. Your blood money will make you rich, but you'll hide in plain sight. You'll pretend to be someone else, and you'll fool most."

I had no idea how she knew about my money—and that concerned me.

"But your life will be a very sad story. Are you sure you want to hear it?"

If I were smart, I would just walk away now. Whether I believed her or not, she was getting inside my head.

When I didn't answer, she continued. "You'll commit unforgivable crimes. You'll kill men when only the Lord should decide who lives and dies. You'll grant life to those who don't deserve it and take life from others who've earned it. As punishment, you'll only love one woman your entire life...but she'll never love you."

I couldn't picture myself loving any woman, no matter how beautiful, how sexy she was between the sheets. With my riches and power, I intended to enjoy every aspect of life, enjoy every woman that would have me.

"This woman will become your wife—but she still won't love you."

I wanted to storm out and call bullshit, but I stayed in my seat, wanting to hear the rest.

"She'll give you two sons—but still won't love you."

I couldn't picture myself being a husband or a father, but I continued to listen.

"You'll be loyal to this woman, protect her with your life, and never take another woman while she's yours—but it will never be enough. Nothing will ever be enough."

"Why would I waste my time on a woman like that?"

She examined the lines in my palm before she let me go. "Because that's the curse. You'll love this woman inexplicably. Forces outside of your control will dictate your emotions. You'll be forced to love her even if you don't want to. That will be your punishment."

"Loving someone doesn't seem like a punishment."

"Love is the most painful feeling in the world. It'll crush you, Hades. To be with the woman you love every day but know she doesn't feel the same way… That's torture."

"Then why would she marry me in the first place?"

She shrugged. "That remains to be foreseen." For the first time since I'd stepped inside that tent, she actually showed emotion—pity. She leaned back against her chair and crossed her arms over her chest, like touching me had burned her fingertips. "But the cards don't lie. You're a dangerous man…and you're only getting started."

"Seriously?" Damien asked as we walked down the pathway to the brothel on the other side of the bazaar. "You're not going to tell me what she said?"

"It was bullshit anyway."

"Then, all the more reason."

"She's just some poor gypsy wanting to take our cash. I'm sure she tried to pickpocket us a few times."

"Didn't look like it to me." He continued to look at me as he walked by my side. "So, what? You're just never going to tell me?"

"If it's bullshit anyway, what does it matter?"

He shrugged. "Maybe it's not bullshit. You never know. She didn't know my name, so she can't be that good."

My feet stopped moving, and I halted in my tracks.

Damien took a few more steps before he realized I'd fallen behind. He turned around and looked at me. "What?"

She knew my name.

Damien hadn't said it all day. There was no way she'd overheard. My driver's license didn't even show that name.

Damien raised an eyebrow. "Everything okay, man?"

I moved forward again, going through the motions even though I was still shocked. "Yeah...I'm fine."

1

SOFIA

IT WAS ONE OF THOSE BIG PARTIES, THE KIND WHERE SO MANY people are invited that you're only going to know a handful of people there. Publicity was important to my parents. As one of the most famous hotel owners in the country, my father had an image to uphold. Success. Popularity. Money. Those were all important to him.

But they were more important to my mother.

It was the grand opening of our new hotel in Florence, Tuscan Rose—with three hundred rooms, a gorgeous lobby, three pools, and everything anyone would want for a summer vacation in Italy.

I was only eighteen years old, but someday, this hotel would be mine. I would run it with the same integrity my father did, with the same attention to detail, and with the best customer service any guest could ask for.

But for tonight, I was still too young to even think about those things. In my black party dress with my hair pulled to one side, I stepped into the ballroom and watched everyone

mingle, holding cocktails as they appreciated the chandeliers hanging from the ceiling, the wagyu beef appetizers
being passed around by the waiters.

I stood off to the side and stared at them all. It was a fun
party, but since I was the youngest person there, I felt out of
place.

My father came out of the crowd, tall, lean, and with a
moustache that he'd sported as long as I could remember,
and placed his hand at the small of my back. "There you are,
Sofia. I wanted to introduce you to a couple people."

I was tired of meeting new people that I would never
remember. Their faces wouldn't register, and their names
would only be in my brain for two seconds before I forgot
them too. I was proud of my father and everything he
accomplished, but I was also bored by the whole ordeal.
"Sure."

He guided me to a group of older men. We shook hands,
exchanged pleasantries, and my father proudly introduced
me as his beautiful daughter. More niceties were exchanged
before they moved away.

Then the most beautiful man in the world walked right up
to us. Young, muscular, and with a light shadow on his
jawline just the way I liked, he approached us both confi-
dently and shook my father's hand. "Congratulations, Peter.
This hotel will be here hundreds of years." He held himself
perfectly straight, a handsome face on a strong frame. His
black suit was nearly the color of his dark hair, and his
brown eyes looked like two pieces of melted chocolate. He
was definitely older than me, but much younger than the
rest of the guests at the party.

When he shifted his gaze to me, my knees grew weak and I felt so damn shy. I was usually a mouthy and sassy girl, but all that attitude disappeared when I came face-to-face with a real man.

He was nothing like the boys I'd liked before.

He was mature wine, aged beef.

I shouldn't even look at him that way. He was too old for me.

The man shifted his gaze to me then extended his hand. "You must be Sofia. Your father has told me so much about you."

It took a few seconds for me to react, to reciprocate his gesture with a handshake.

He squeezed my hand hard, and then let go.

"It's nice to meet you too," I forced myself to say.

His eyes lingered on mine for a moment longer before he turned back to my father. "Lovely party. I expect we'll be here all night."

"I hope so. I paid for a lot of booze, so we'd better drink it all." He chuckled then looked at me. "This fine young man is making a name for himself in the finance world. I suspect he'll be a big asset to us in a few years."

"Yes," he said. "You're probably right." He politely excused himself. "Have a good evening, Mr. Romano."

"You too." When he was gone, my father turned back to me. "Having a good time, Sofia?"

I'd been pretty bored...until he showed up. "Yeah...I think I am."

I TRIED NOT to make my stare obvious, but it seemed like every time I looked at that hot man, he was already looking at me.

So he caught my stare.

I combated the redness in my cheeks as much as possible, but no amount of foundation could keep the color at bay. My eyes drifted to a table where a pack of cigarettes lay, an unguarded lighter there as well. The fact that there were so many people in the room actually made it easy to sneak around and get away with anything, so I grabbed a cigarette, lit it, and then walked outside.

It was late, so the balcony was deserted. The distant sound of voices carried through the windows and thudded against my eardrums. Every bit of laughter was obnoxious because it was so fake.

That was why I hated these events.

Publicity stunts.

I leaned against the wall, out of sight, and enjoyed my cigarette, my arms crossed and one foot planted against the wall. From the top story of the hotel, I had a prime view of Florence, the lights brilliant and beautiful. A breeze was in the air, and it licked at the sweat that formed on the back of my neck. Being separated from the herd was nice because I wouldn't be tempted to stare at that sexy man.

The sexy man who was way out of my league.

I continued to pull the smoke into my lungs and let it drift from my nostrils. My parents had no idea I smoked, but they were aware I loved wine more than they did. With every drag of nicotine, I became calmer, tapping my finger against the tip so the ashes would fall to the floor.

My wrist relaxed as my head rested against the wall, feeling the fatigue settle into my bones when I realized it must be one in the morning by now. The crowd continued to party, but it couldn't last much longer.

I'd only closed my eyes for a few seconds when the cigarette was ripped from my fingers.

Shit. I'd been caught.

My eyes opened and settled on the man who had stolen my attention since the moment I'd laid eyes on him.

He brought the cigarette to his lips, took a deep drag, and let the smoke drift away with the breeze. "You don't strike me as a smoker."

My heart raced a million miles an hour in my chest, and I lost all my confidence in the blink of an eye. This man made me so nervous, I could barely breathe, let alone think of a comeback. "Occasionally."

"Occasionally is just as bad as regularly."

"I don't see why."

"Either one takes years off your life." He took another drag from my cigarette then looked over the edge of the balcony to the city below. The smoke lifted from his lips, and he looked so sexy standing there.

"Maybe you should take your own advice."

He shrugged. "I don't plan to live long."

I extended my hand. "Can I have it back?" Even if it was just to feel the moisture of his mouth against the tip of that cigarette. It was like a dirty kiss, nicotine and smoke mixed in between.

"No." He crushed it within his palm without wincing then threw it in the garbage can.

"That was rude."

"I'm an asshole, so no surprise there." He stood with his body perpendicular to mine and stared at the marvelous view from our fancy party. His hands slid into the pockets of his suit as he enjoyed the fresh air with me.

I did my best to play it cool. "Are you going to tell my father?"

"I'm not a rat." He slowly turned his gaze back to me, his brown eyes inexplicably pretty. He seemed too handsome to be true, like Prince Charming in a fairy tale. He'd been a lot nicer inside, but now he seemed moody, off-putting. But he continued to linger there anyway...as if he wanted to be with me.

"Thanks. But you could have given me back that cigarette."

"Trust me, I'm looking out for you." He stepped up next to me, bringing us close together so we could drop our voices further. If someone came outside, they would see us in deep conversation and probably assume something inappropriate was happening. But no one was going to come out here at this time of night, at least, I hoped not. I'd dated guys while in school, but I'd never had a serious boyfriend. Now that I was officially an adult about to start business school at the university, I expected that to change.

Maybe it would change tonight.

"I don't need someone to look out for me." I kept my arms crossed over my chest and leaned against the wall, feigning indifference. But something told me this man could see right through that. "How do you know my father?"

"We do business together." He didn't elaborate further. Maybe he thought his job was boring and didn't want to drone on about it.

That was unfortunate because I genuinely wanted to know. "One day, I'm going to take over for my father and run this hotel."

"Ambitious...I like that."

I tried to hide my smile, but the corner of my lip raised slightly.

"Nothing sexier than a woman knowing what she wants." His voice was deep like dark chocolate. It rumbled in his throat before it emerged, sweet on the ears. This man looked beautiful, sounded beautiful...he just was beautiful.

"Do you know what you want?"

He turned his gaze toward me, his jawline hard as if it were chiseled from stone. "Yes. I take ambition a little too far."

Bumps appeared on my arms even though it was still humid and warm. My nipples pressed against the cups of my bra, and I resisted the urge to fidget. This was the first man who had made me feel passion and lust, the kind they showed in books and movies. The other boys I'd been interested in were practically friends. This guy was...a man. "I never got your name."

He slowly turned back to the balcony. "Hades."

I couldn't control the eyebrow that rose up my face. "That's your name?"

"Yes. Not as beautiful as Sofia, but it will do."

"Isn't that the god of the underworld?"

"Yes, to those who believe in Greek mythology. Are you one of those people?"

"No. But it's still an interesting name."

He was standoffish and cold, staring at the view of the city that was practically laid at our feet. Even with his hands in his pockets, he stood perfectly straight, having a strong back and an ass that looked great in those slacks. He wore a shiny watch. "It's a name you don't forget easily." He turned away and headed back to the doorway without saying goodbye.

I didn't want him to go. He was the first interesting person I'd met at the party, and I wasn't eager to lose my only friend...and whatever else I wanted him to be. "Going to steal more cigarettes?"

He stopped and slowly turned, a touch of amusement in his eyes. He came back toward me, taking his time because he knew I wasn't going anywhere. "Taking cigarettes isn't exactly a hobby."

"Fooled me. So, will I see you around?"

His eyes shifted back and forth slightly as they looked into mine. "Do you want to see me around, Sofia?"

The way he said my name caused chills to run down my spine. Boys would make up a lie and walk away, but this was a man who got right to the point. He wasn't afraid to confront me, to make me uncomfortable with that deep stare.

I wanted to respond with some smartass comment, but I didn't want to play games. This man wasn't playing games with me, so why should I play games with him? "Yes."

A minor look of surprise came into his gaze at my honesty. His lips pressed together a bit as he continued to look at me, as if some internal argument made him clench his entire body. His eyes were open, and he hardly blinked as he stared at me. "You're a beautiful girl, Sofia. One day, you're going to be a gorgeous woman. Maybe then you'll see me around." He put me down gently, but it still hurt.

I didn't expect anything from him, but knowing he would walk away and I would probably never see him again was a huge disappointment. The first man I'd actually felt some heat for was out of my league. "How old are you?"

He grinned, showing his natural charm. "Too old."

I hadn't lifted my body from the wall. So far, I'd managed to get him to stay with just my words. But eventually, he would walk away, and words wouldn't be enough to keep him close. "And how old is too old?"

He came closer to me, his shoulder making contact with the wall. His voice lowered to a whisper. "Twenty-five."

That meant he was seven years older than me. He had seven more years of experience, seven more years of women in his bed.

And I hadn't taken anyone to bed.

He watched my reaction. "Like I said, too old." He turned away, dismissing our conversation for good.

I would leave for university in Milan in a few months, so I suspected I would never see this man again. I was a new adult who was flooded with hormones, and I wanted a real kiss, a real experience that would make me feel like a woman. This man was the first one who turned me on, who made me want to take off my clothes and get rid of my virginity. But he wouldn't be around for that.

So I grabbed him by the arm and pulled him into me. Knowing this could never be more, that this could never be anything but a secret, I put myself on the line and dug my fingers into his hair as I kissed him.

Instead of pulling away, he kissed me back. He smiled slightly against my mouth as he pressed me farther into the wall, his hard body so strong against my softness. "Alright, baby. Just one." His hand slid into the back of my hair, and he angled my head up so he could kiss me hard. His warm breath filled my mouth, and the hard outline of his dick pressed right into my stomach. He gave me his tongue, gave me his passion.

I took it all. My hands snaked up his back, and I held him close to me, wanting to feel something real instead of the stagnant fakeness my family exuded. I didn't have the perfect family like everyone believed. My parents didn't love each other. Sometimes I wasn't sure if they even loved me.

But this was real.

It was wrong, so wrong, that Hades could be shot if he got

caught pressed up against me, but he kissed me like he didn't have a care in the world. With his back turned to everything else but us, he grabbed my thigh and wrapped it around his hips, thrusting his package into the perfect spot between my legs.

Oh yes...

He stopped our kiss so he could watch my reaction, see the way I responded to the friction.

I liked it...a lot. "Ooh..."

His hand remained fisted in my hair. "Has a man ever made you come, baby?"

I was so embarrassed that I wanted to lie, but when I looked into those brown eyes, I knew I had to say nothing but the truth. "No..."

His lips moved to mine again, and he kissed me slowly, grinding up against me in the nighttime air. I could feel the wetness in my panties, and he could probably feel them against his slacks at that point. Every kiss was dynamite. Every kiss was fire. I'd never been kissed so good, never had my toes curl so hard. Was this what it always felt like? Was this the kind of heat every couple felt?

He ground harder and harder, my dress sliding up farther as he rubbed into me. He sucked my bottom lip into his mouth then gave me another thrust.

A thrust that made me so white-hot, I thought someone had set me on fire. Whimpers escaped my lips, and I wanted to scream until my lungs gave out.

He kept his mouth over mine and muffled the noise, letting me finish my climax without fear.

It was so good.

Euphoric.

God, I wanted to do that again.

He kissed me a few more times before he pulled away, slightly out of breath with tousled hair. He kept his face close to mine, his breathing deep and quiet. "You're a virgin." He didn't phrase it as a question, as if he already knew the answer without asking.

I didn't correct him.

"Can I give you some advice?"

I gave a slight nod.

"In a few years, every man in the world is going to chase you. But most men are assholes. Most men will treat you like garbage and throw you away. Don't let them. Don't waste your time on someone who doesn't deserve you. You're a beautiful woman with a powerful surname. Don't be one of those girls who lets losers fuck her. Be that woman who only lets a king fuck her."

"Are you a king?" I blurted, my words coming out as a whisper.

His eyes shifted back and forth as he held on to my gaze. "I am *the* king."

2

SOFIA

FOUR YEARS LATER

I LIFTED MY SUITCASE ONTO MY OLD BED THEN OPENED THE lid. Stacks of jeans, tops, and dresses were inside, all the things I wore while I was at university in Milan. For four years, I studied business and poetry. I learned everything I possibly could about running a business, operating a company that was ethical, that treated its employees with dignity, and how to keep a business open for decades.

My family owned a chain of hotels throughout Italy, ranging from the toe of the boot in the south all the way to the north close to Nice, France. As an only child, I was the heir to take over the family business.

I intended to make our hotels outlive our family by many generations. I was best acquainted with the hotel in Milan since I'd been studying there for the last four years, but the hotel in Florence was my favorite. I witnessed my father build it from the ground up, making his dream into a reality with such calm suavity. I never told him how proud I was of his work, and now that he was dead, I regretted it every single day of my life.

Now I was back in Florence, moving back in with my mother until I found my own footing. Living alone for the last few years had given me a taste of independence that I didn't want to relinquish. I'd lived in a small apartment, but I'd had the freedom to eat cereal before bed, have men spend the night, and let my laundry pile up until it was a behemoth on the floor in the corner of my room. My booze and cigarettes could be enjoyed without a judgmental gaze.

My mother lived with my stepfather in the same mansion where I grew up, three stories right in the heart of the city. It wasn't like we wouldn't have the privacy we needed from one another.

But still, a grown woman shouldn't be living with her mother.

I finished unpacking then went out onto the terrace on the second floor, where we had breakfast every morning in the summer before it got too hot. It was almost fall, so the temperature was somewhat diminishing. The humidity was taking a little longer.

Mother sat there, her legs crossed, a cigarette resting between her soft fingertips. She had dark brown hair just like mine, perfectly styled to maintain her beauty. She still had beautiful skin, her wrinkles hidden under all the products she used to fight the detrimental effects of aging.

With my eyebrow raised, I approached her from behind and snatched the cigarette from her poised hand. "Things have changed around here."

She maintained her calm posture, her eyes following my movements as I took the seat beside her. A cup of coffee was on the table next to her hand, just black even though she preferred cream and sugar. "Not really. I just don't bother to hide it anymore."

"Smoking takes years off your life." Anytime I felt a cigarette between my fingertips, I thought of the erotic night I'd had on a balcony four years ago. A man took it right out of my hand and tossed it away.

"I don't care." She opened the pack and pulled out another.

"It causes wrinkles…"

She had the cigarette in her mouth with the lighter held close to the tip. Instead of striking it with her thumb and making it burst into flame, she sighed and put everything down.

"That's what I thought." That was the kind of woman my mother was. She cared more about her appearance than living a long, healthy life.

"Don't be so prissy. I've found your stash around the house."

I didn't deny it. They said mothers knew everything. They were right.

A servant brought me a cup of coffee, but I didn't hesitate before I added cream and sugar. I liked it fattening, packed with sweetness and calories, and I didn't give a damn about the destruction to my waistline. "I quit a few years ago."

"Why?"

"Because I want to live past forty."

"Now that's an exaggeration." Instead of reaching for her cigarettes, she grabbed her coffee and took a sip. She examined the view before us, the sun rising over the beautiful city, highlighting the green hillsides in the background. Even from miles away, the scent of grapes was always in the air. "How does it feel to be home?"

"It's nice..."

She chuckled. "You hate it, don't you?"

"I'm just not thrilled to be moving back in with my mother."

"I lived with my parents until I got married."

"But you got married when you were nineteen."

She shrugged. "There's nothing to be ashamed of. Soon enough, the same will happen to you."

I didn't have any interest in getting married. I loved my parents, but their marriage was depressing. My mother's second marriage to my stepfather was even worse. My mother only gave herself to a man for one reason—to be taken care of. She wanted a man to handle the business, the finances, and be the alpha in the relationship.

That sounded like mindless slavery to me.

I had much bigger ambitions in life. "I'm going to work with Gustavo tomorrow. He's gonna show me a few things about the hotel, give me a job so I can learn as much as possible." It never made sense to me that my mother remarried and handed her position in her business to her new husband. That just seemed stupid to me.

She slowly turned to me, not even bothering to cover the disdain in her eyes. "Honey, men are supposed to work. Women make other people work for them."

"It's not just a random job. I want to take over the hotel business when Gustavo retires."

"Your husband can handle that."

I loved my mother, but her old-fashioned outlook on marriage was so archaic that she seemed senile. "Maybe that was true a hundred years ago, but things have changed. I'm perfectly capable of handling our company on my own."

"I know you're a bright girl with a lot of brilliant ideas. But it doesn't matter how smart you are. It doesn't mean you can get things done."

My fingers rested on the top of my coffee cup, the heat reaching my skin. Even simple conversations with my mother turned into wars on a battlefield. She was so stubborn and opinionated that even mundane discussions were unbearable. "What's that supposed to mean?"

"It means..." She took a sip of her coffee then set it down beside her. "That no matter how hard you try, people will never respect you the way they would respect a man. They won't listen to you or value your ideas. Anytime you delegate, they'll assume you're being an overbearing bitch. People will push you around and take advantage of you. That's just the world we live in...which is why you need a powerful husband who can protect your wealth and interests."

It was such a load of horseshit. "If you really believe that, why did you encourage me to attend university?"

"To get your M-R-S. Degree."

"Excuse me?" I asked, an eyebrow raised.

"I wanted you to meet a good man and settle down. But you came back without a ring on your finger."

"I wasn't shopping for a husband. I was only interested in learning."

She shrugged then kept looking out at the breathtaking view. Most people would never know the wealth we got to enjoy—and we didn't even work for it. "You're still young, so enjoy yourself, Sofia. Date men you'll never marry. Screw guys who will only hold your interest for a night. Because eventually...all that fun stuff ends. That's one of my regrets... not enjoying my youth. I immediately married your father... I wish I'd let loose first."

I'd definitely been letting loose, and the casual detachment was simple. Maybe if I met a man I really liked, things would be different. But the idea of settling down into boring mediocrity sounded terrible. I wanted to be an executive, I wanted to have flings, and I wanted to have a family some-day...even if I did it on my own. But being tied down to one man forever...sounded terrible. "I'm only twenty-two. I have a lot of youth left inside me."

"Then enjoy it. But don't get your hopes up about running that hotel."

The sexism surprised me, especially coming from my own mother. "It's nice to be home."

She chuckled, picking up on my sarcasm. "I can't wait for you to move out either."

GUSTAVO HAD MARRIED my mother just three months after my father was gone.

He was a widower, having lost his wife in a terrible car accident just a few years before my father died. He had one son, who lived out of the house and had already started his own family. I didn't know the specifics of my mother's second nuptials, but I knew it had been negotiated like a contract.

But in any case, I liked him.

He was kind, affectionate, and treated my mom well. When I saw them together, they seemed more like friends than man and wife. Maybe that was why their relationship worked so well. My mother wanted a man to take care of her, and Gustavo didn't want to be lonely.

It could be worse, so I let it be.

We went to the Tuscan Rose together and entered the lobby. Several chandeliers hung from the ceiling, the crystals on fire as the light shone through the prisms. White vases with fresh flowers lined the tables and counters, and mirrors on the wall showed how expansive the room really was. I loved the energy the second I stepped inside, loved the excitement of the guests as they checked in at the front desk. It was impeccably clean, a visual representation of the Romano family name.

"I suggest you start with a concierge position." Instead of leading me to the back where the offices were located, he stopped in the lobby. "You know so much about this city, and you're so good with people. It's a great start."

I looked up at him in surprise, finding no comfort in the warm look he gave me. He was a tall man, taller than my father had been, and his dark skin showed his exotic origins. He wore eyeglasses on the bridge of his nose. In conversation, he was a polite and restrained man, but when his eyes lit up with warmth, he was a whole new person. "I'm not interested in the concierge position. I was hoping to shadow you, to look at the bookkeeping, and take on whatever other managerial positions I can assist with."

His smile never faded. "I realize that, but—"

"Don't listen to my mother. I know how she feels about this, but this is my legacy, and I intend to hold on to it." I wouldn't get married just to have another man control my company. I didn't need anyone's assistance but my own.

His smile slowly faded. "This is her hotel, Sofia. I don't have a lot of say in the matter."

"You obviously do if you're running it." I stood my ground and refused to back down. I would only get what I wanted in life if I fought for it. It didn't make sense that my mother's second husband got to manage what belonged to our family. It should either be my mother or me.

He sighed as he lowered his gaze. "I was under the impression you needed money."

"Yes. I've got to move out as quickly as possible."

He chuckled. "I can imagine. But I can't offer you a position as a manager or anything of that nature. You had excellent marks at university, but experience is more important in an occupation like this. You'll have to start at the bottom."

"I never said I had a problem with that." I didn't expect to be given everything just because of my last name, but I did expect the chance to prove my worthiness. "I'll take the concierge position if you teach me everything about running this hotel. I can work with you in the morning and take the concierge position in the evenings."

"You mean business, don't you?"

"Always." I placed one hand on my hip, looking up at my stepfather without budging an inch. I refused to let this go without at least fighting for it. Maybe the concierge job would pay enough to cover my rent, and with enough time, I would prove to my stepfather and mother that I was capable of taking over when the time was right.

Gustavo was the man in the relationship, but he possessed much more compassion than she ever did. He didn't seem to harbor the same sexist viewpoint she did. "Alright. Let's keep this between us—for now."

I moved into his chest and hugged him. "Thank you, Gustavo. It means so much to me."

GUSTAVO HAD an office and a conference room off to the side of the hotel. There were several other offices belonging to personnel involved with the daily operations of the hotel. One office was empty, and a nameplate wasn't attached to the door.

I worked with Gustavo for the day, shadowing his move-ments and understanding the duties of a manager of the hotel. Technically, he had a general manager who oversaw the employees, but he was responsible for the financial aspect. I got to study the balance sheets, seeing how much money the hotel earned on a daily basis. It was impressive—especially during the off-season.

The hours passed quickly, and I couldn't help but assume my mother was an idiot. Man or woman, it didn't matter. Anyone could run this hotel if they were passionate about it. I wanted to tell my mother to return to ancient times, because the present didn't suit her well.

Gustavo printed off a few spreadsheets then laid them across the desk. "I have a meeting in just a few minutes. How about you focus on this until I'm finished?"

"What's the meeting about?"

"Money," he said, half joking. "Everything is always about money." He was just about to step outside when a man appeared in the doorway. Tall, muscular, and wearing a suit like a second skin, he wasn't the kind of guest I expected... because he was so young.

I was sitting at the desk, my eyes taking in the man in the gray suit. With brown eyes that seemed both dangerous and warm, he had a familiar face. He had high cheekbones and a masculine tightness to his features, and his appearance immediately ran a bell. It'd been so many years since I'd last seen him that I almost didn't recognize him.

He'd been a man the last time I saw him. But now...he was a bigger man.

With broad shoulders and tight forearms, his manly physique was noticeable through his clothes. A shiny watch was on his wrist, an Omega, probably worth tens of thousands of euros. His thumb casually brushed over his bottom lip as he entered, his chin covered with a thick shadow that hadn't been shaved in days. The cords in his neck were distinct, especially since his skin was tanned and tight. He had full lips, perfect for a hot kiss in the darkness of a cold bedroom. Those eyes were so powerful, they could make a woman spread her knees in just seconds.

I'd had some decent lovers in Milan...but none of them had looked like this man.

Hades.

He addressed my stepfather first. "Gustavo."

My stepfather walked over to him and shook his hand. "Thanks for coming by. I know you're a busy man."

"A man is never too busy to make money." It was the first time his eyes turned to me, and without his giving any significant reaction, it was clear he recognized me. It was the subtle narrowing of his eyes, the slight clench of his hard jaw. Slowly, his hands returned to his pockets as he studied me.

When we'd first met, I was nothing but a shy girl. I was barely an adult and didn't possess the courage to handle an experienced man. His confidence had unnerved me, made me back up against the wall and turn rigid with fear.

But not anymore.

I rose to my feet and glided to him, working my heels like they were comfortable sandals. With my hand outstretched, I greeted him like he was a business associate. "Nice to see you again, Hades."

He didn't pull his hand out of his pocket for a second, as if my offer were inappropriate. Our first meeting had been anything but professional. We were two walking hormones who ground up against the wall like it was our last night on earth. I still thought about that climax sometimes, the first one of its kind. It was powerful, profound, and so much better than the pathetic ones the boys had given me.

He finally took my hand. His fingers moved all the way to my wrist, and he immediately squeezed me firmly, the pressure making my blood circulate from both fear and arousal. His eyes never left mine, and he didn't seem to care if my stepfather picked up on the heat between us. "I'm sorry about your father. He was a good man." It didn't feel like a false sentiment. My father had been dead for years, and Hades didn't need to acknowledge it. Seemed like he meant it.

I dropped the handshake first. "Thank you."

"Good, you're acquainted." Gustavo gave me a gentle pat on the back before he stepped through the doorway and into the hallway. "Hades and I will take an hour, maybe more."

"Can I sit in?" I asked, knowing he would say no.

"Not today," Gustavo said. "In time." He rounded the corner.

Hades lingered for a second longer, letting his eyes take me in as if he could easily picture me naked. Innate confidence burned in his eyes, as if nothing and no one could ever make him question who he was. He took a gentle step back, not wanting to take his eyes off me. Then he finally turned around.

My eyes immediately went to his ass.

Still tight, I saw.

3

SOFIA

I DIDN'T SEE HADES AGAIN.

I wasn't entirely sure what business he had with Gustavo. He mentioned something about working in finance a long time ago, but I couldn't recall the specifics. Maybe he never even told me that information…I just assumed. When I asked Gustavo, all he said was, "He handles the money."

That didn't make sense.

I was determined to be a respected member of the team at Tuscan Rose, so I wouldn't get involved with someone who was also on the payroll, not that I assumed anything would happen in the first place. That kiss had been four years ago, and we were complete strangers. Perhaps he'd been just as bored at that party as I was, so he followed me just to get away from the stiffness.

I could feel embarrassed by our past, but I refused. It was one moment, one night. Nothing much to say about it. He was even sexier than I remembered, so I couldn't pretend that he wasn't a walking piece of eye candy. He was gorgeous...plain and simple. But gorgeous men were only good for one thing.

Fucking.

I started my shift in the concierge department that evening, helping American guests decide where to make dinner reservations in this historic town. Most of them were newly-weds, so their excitement was palpable. I also booked a few spa treatments, and by nine, I finally got to walk out the door.

Instead of heading home...to my mother's...I decided to go out instead. I had a couple friends in Florence, and after a few texts, we met somewhere crowded and dark, going straight for the hard liquor and skipping the wine.

I had wine for breakfast. It was practically water to me at this point.

"How's the new job?" Esme had blonde hair and blue eyes, looking nothing like me but definitely more beautiful. She wore a white dress with a black blazer on top, finished with her job at the art gallery.

"It's gonna pay my bills, so it's pretty good."

She chuckled. "Are you in training to take over?"

"Yes and no. Right now, I'm just shadowing my stepfather and doing a few small tasks."

"Not a bad way to get paid." She had a scotch—neat. Her nails were painted fiery red, which was an interesting color against her fair skin.

"I actually don't get paid for that. That's all volunteer."

"Then how do you plan to pay your bills…?" She cocked an eyebrow as she took a drink. "You got a sugar daddy?"

"No. I work the concierge gig in the evenings."

"Oh…not nearly as exciting as having a sugar daddy."

I chuckled. "No. Not even close."

"What's it like so far? Do you help a lot of hot businessmen taking their mistresses to their rooms?"

"No. I'm sure they would be more secretive than to stop by for a chat. They don't care about eating the best pasta or visiting the Barsetti winery for wine tasting. All they care about is fucking and getting room service."

"Ooh…" A dreamy look came into her eyes. "Sex and room service. That sounds like a dream."

"It does." It'd been a while since I'd had a good man between the sheets. My lovers were casual, nothing serious because I hadn't intended to stay in Milan for more than a couple of years. Being a student was a good way to meet new people, especially men my own age. But I'd never had a deeply passionate relationship, the kind where you couldn't keep your hands off each other for more than a few minutes. Maybe that was love. Or maybe that was combustive lust.

"Are you seeing anyone?"

"Me?" I asked incredulously. "No. Not while I'm still living with my mother."

"How's that going?"

"It's not terrible. I mean, we have so much space, it's not like we're fighting to use the bathroom or the washing machine.

It's just weird to live under her roof again, like I'm a child or a failed adult. I miss bringing men home. I can't do that anymore."

"I'm sure you could sneak one in."

"Eh...don't really want to do that." That would make me seem dishonest and childish.

"Couldn't you just stay at his place?"

"I suppose. But then my mother will wonder where I've been all night."

"No, she'll know where you've been all night," she said with a smile. "You're a grown woman, so I doubt she'll give you a hard time about it."

"Yeah..." My mother was a very blunt person, and she even encouraged me to enjoy my youth as much as possible, be with all the men who would never be my husband, get it out of my system before I settled down with a suitable partner. "She probably wouldn't care. Probably wouldn't ask me any questions. But I guess it's just awkward giving her an idea of what I'm doing in my private life."

"I always thought the two of you were close." Esme was oblivious to all the attention she was capturing. Lots of men behind her wouldn't stop staring at her, probably trying to decide if they should buy her a drink or just walk up and talk to her.

"We are. I love my mother. We just don't see eye to eye on a lot of things. When my father passed away, we became a lot closer." My parents were never in love, but it was obvious my mother's sadness at his passing was genuine. She'd lost a friend...a partner.

One of the men who had his eyes on Esme finally made his move. Tall and handsome, he had a nice smile and shoulders built for strength. He appeared on her right side, his hands in his pockets so he wouldn't seem overly eager. "Hello, I'm Kyle." He extended his hand to shake hers.

When her eyes widened in approval, I knew she liked what she saw. "Esme." She shook his hand. "This is my friend Sofia."

He shook my hand. "Lovely to meet you both."

They became engaged in conversation, making each other laugh and exchanging subtle cues of affection.

I silently excused myself so my friend could get laid. I brought my drink to another table and took a seat. Sitting alone anywhere besides the bar was awkward, but I wasn't ready to end my evening just yet. I wanted to enjoy this last bit of vodka cranberry before I walked home.

My eyes wandered around the bar, people-watching. There were a few packs of women at the bar, gathered close together and chatting over a bottle of wine. A lot of the men were looking in their direction.

But some were looking at me.

I didn't see anyone I was interested in, so I kept my gaze averted.

My eyes scanned to the left, and they stopped immediately when I noticed a man I recognized. Sitting in a dark booth facing the rest of the bar, he wore a white shirt with black slacks and dress shoes. With his jacket missing, the hardness of his body was unmistakable. His pecs were easy to visualize, and he had such strong shoulders that they stretched the fabric of his shirt and made it tight. His tanned skin contrasted against the white fabric of his shirt, making him look worshiped by the sun. His head was turned slightly toward the woman beside him, a brunette who squeezed his thigh under the table and whispered into his ear.

Her blue eyes were glued to his side profile, her eyes heavy with lust and affection. She looked at that man like he was all she wanted in this world, like she wanted to take him home and never let him leave. Her hand grazed right over his crotch then slowly moved up his chest, pampering him as she slid toward his neck.

Hades had his arm around her shoulders, but he didn't shower her in the same affection. He looked at her indirectly and allowed her to touch him, to let her claim him as hers. She was a beautiful woman a man would give up anything to be with, but to him, she didn't seem that important.

She moved her body into him, pressing her tits against his arm and chest as she whispered something into his ear.

He grinned when he heard whatever dirty thing she'd just said.

I hardly knew Hades, so I couldn't make assumptions about his character, but from what I was watching, he was like every other handsome and successful man. He was in the game indefinitely, never retiring his jersey. She was just another notch on his bedpost.

But to her, she thought she'd won the jackpot.

I'd been a victim of that handsome grin, of those pretty eyes that made you melt. I'd only spoken to him for minutes when I'd dug my fingers into his hair and yanked him against me. He oozed masculinity, and he reeked of good sex. I told myself I was a young girl giving in to my hormones, but I still felt the same level of attraction toward him now. He was a safe bet, a man who wouldn't take you home then let you down.

I continued to enjoy my drink and watch them, wishing I were going home with a hunk myself. It was nice to wash off the workday with a glass of booze, but getting fucked by a big dick was better.

Hades eventually turned away from her and looked around, probably intending to order another drink since his was empty. It only took him a second to notice me sitting alone in the black leather booth. His jaw didn't tighten, and his eyes didn't narrow in recognition. He had no reaction at all —a perfect poker face.

Once our eyes had locked for several seconds, I turned away and kept nursing my drink. When the waitress came by, I would close my tab and head home. Esme was gonna score with a handsome guy, and the last man I'd had an erotic encounter with in Florence was just feet away from me, another woman about to give him a hand job under the table. I should just call it quits and head home.

From the corner of my eye, I saw Hades have a brief conversation with his date then slide out of the booth. When he stood, the air in the room changed, a spark had been ignited. He moved down the stairs and came toward me.

I took a long drink from my glass and ignored him.

He invited himself into my leather booth, sliding in until he was close beside me.

I couldn't help but take a peek at the woman he'd been with just seconds ago. She watched him turn his attention on me with fire in her gaze. She looked equally enraged and hurt.

He sat beside me, his body pivoted toward me with one arm on the table. His silver watch was visible just underneath the sleeve of his collared shirt. He smelled like sandalwood and smoke, like he was a man who spent his time outdoors in the forest. Silence passed between us, the music from the speakers not loud enough to fill the void in conversation.

I refused to speak first, so I continued to drink like he wasn't there.

Hades wasn't unnerved by my indifference. He continued to stare at me, comfortable with the unspoken feud raging between us. His brown eyes watched my movements, watched me sip from my glass then return it to the table. Every movement I made was observed.

Now, I started to become uncomfortable, started to break under that formidable stare. But I refuse to give any indication that I was tense, that I was the same shy girl he'd met four years ago.

To break the ice, I pushed my glass toward him.

He lifted the glass, shook the ice, and then took a drink. He set it down and slid it back toward me. "Piss."

"Better than what you're drinking."

"I'm not drinking anything."

I held up my glass. "Exactly." I took another drink and

watched Esme get lost in her conversation with her new friend. She didn't seem to notice that I'd disappeared. She was probably so smitten with the guy that everything else ceased to matter.

The corner of his mouth rose in a smile, just slightly. Then he subtly raised his hand and immediately got the attention of the waiter. Without looking at him, he ordered. "Scotch, neat, double."

The waiter ran off, fetched the drink, and then set it on the table.

Hades slid it toward me then gave a slight nod.

Just to prove a point, I took a drink without making a sour face, and then slid it back to him. "Piss."

This time, both corners of his mouth rose in a smile.

I drank from my glass a little more often than usual, feeling the nerves getting to me. I assumed he would say a couple of words then return to his date, but he continued to linger like his agenda hadn't been fulfilled.

"My assumption was incorrect." He swirled his glass and took another drink. "You are far more beautiful than I ever could have predicted." This man was confident enough to speak his mind without fear of the consequences, to tell a woman she was beautiful without being afraid of her response. The sting of rejection had never pierced his skin, so he didn't carry scars like the rest of us.

I shouldn't be flattered by that comment, but in all honesty, I was. "Am I still too young for you?" I could still smell the nighttime air on my nose, feel the bumps on my arms, the taste of smoke in my mouth. It was a lifetime ago, when I was a completely different person, but it all came rushing back to me. At the time, our age difference didn't matter. He was a gorgeous man that I'd wanted to sink my claws into. I'd assumed I was an adult that could handle anything. But now that I was older, I knew he'd made the right call when he walked away. He gave in to a moment of weakness and kissed me, but he didn't let it grow into something else. He really was too old for me... We both knew it.

He set his glass down and let his deep-brown eyes look into mine, piercing my gaze as if he could see everything underneath my skin. He could see my heartbeat, my damaged soul. He could see the curves of my body through my tight dress, notice the sharpness of my tits. He slowly brought his hand to his mouth and dragged his fingers across his lips, as if he were catching a drop of scotch that somehow had missed his tongue. He was clearly uncomfortable in the tense silence between words. It was as if he fed off the heat. "Definitely not." His eyes lowered slightly, giving me a quick glance-over before he lifted his eyes to meet my gaze again. One hand grasped his glass while the other stayed on his thigh.

The lock between our gazes started to make me sweat. He was better at this game than I was, so I took a drink to wash away the tension in the cords of my neck. All my muscles tightened painfully, making me rigid. I vowed I would never let a man affect my confidence, but Hades was an opponent I could never beat.

"Following in your father's footsteps?"

"Trying to."

"Still ambitious, I see." He glanced around the bar, his eyes gently scanning his surroundings for nothing in particular. "That's sexy in a woman."

"Sexy in a man, too."

He turned back to me. "Then you won't be able to keep your hands off me."

"I'm doing it right now."

He grinned slightly. "Give it time."

I wanted to destroy his confidence, but I couldn't because he was right. Just like with every other woman in the world, this man had me. He'd already watched me yank him into my arms and kiss him while my family could catch us at any moment. My cards were already on the table.

"Take my advice?" He rubbed his thumb against his glass, wiping away the condensation.

"About getting fucked?" I asked bluntly.

He gave a slight nod.

"That's a personal question, and it's none of your business."

"It is my business." He turned to me, freezing me in place with that serious look. His brown eyes were beautiful in that masculine face, his dark hair around his jaw, the beautiful structure of his countenance... Everything made him perfect. "Because I'm going to fuck you."

The second he said the last word, my heart spiked and started to pulse like I was about to sprint a marathon. Sweat formed at the back of my neck when I imagined his perfect body on top of mine, making good on his word. I would resist at first, pretending that every thrust he gave wasn't the best sex I'd ever had, but when he made me come, it would be impossible to lie. He would push me until I admitted the truth...that I wanted him inside me again and again. I'd never felt that way with another man, as if I couldn't get enough of him and wanted him in my bed every night. I suspected Hades would be the first, and that told me I should stay away from him. "That's presumptuous."

"Am I wrong?" He turned his body closer to mine, bringing us in such proximity that we must look like lovers to everyone in the room, like two people who'd been fucking for weeks.

Past his shoulder, I could see the woman still sitting there, watching Hades press his advances on a different woman. She'd been the focus of his attention until the moment he'd laid eyes on me, and she probably couldn't figure out what went wrong. Seeing her pain and confusion made me feel guilty for being the other woman, for essentially stealing him away. "Yes."

His eyes softened slightly, like that was an answer he'd never imagined I would give.

"You should get back to your girl, Hades. She's waiting for you." I opened my clutch and fished out cash to leave on the table.

He didn't look over his shoulder. "I don't have a girl."

"The woman you were with just minutes ago."

"She's not my girl. Just met her."

"Well, ignoring her and pursuing someone else is rude." I slid out of the booth and didn't look back as I walked away. I didn't care if he was a playboy. I didn't care if he would fuck someone else the night after he fucked me. It was none of my business. But I wasn't interested in a man who could be so mercilessly rude. I walked outside and started the journey home.

He emerged behind me minutes later, as if he'd debated coming after me before he rose from his seat. His loud foot-steps were audible on the cement behind me, his dress shoes giving a distinct tap that I recognized.

He moved in front of me and cut off my path. On his feet and in front of me, he was a big man, bigger than he was when he was sitting beside me in the booth. He was over a foot taller than me and with a muscle mass that made mine pathetic. He could squish me if he wanted to, choke me with a single hand and leave me for dead on the sidewalk. His eyes quickly shifted back and forth as he looked into my gaze, like he was livid with the way I'd walked away from him.

I bet no one ever walked away from him.

"I'm not done with you."

"Well, I'm done with you." I stepped around him.

He grabbed me by the arm and forced me back.

I twisted out of his grasp and stepped back. "Touch me again, and see what happens."

My tough threat only made him smile. It was a slight grin, where only one corner of his mouth lifted. "I'd love that, actually. But I'm a gentleman...for the most part." He slid his hands into his pockets, as if he wanted to prove his sincerity. "Come over."

I'd never met a man so arrogant in my life. "Why would I want to come home with you?"

"So we don't have to finish this conversation on the sidewalk."

"There's no conversation to finish."

His smile faded away, and his eyes turned hostile once more. "I met that girl ten minutes before I noticed you sitting there. I don't owe her a damn thing. If I hadn't seen you across the bar, I probably would have taken her home and fucked her. But I saw you...and I'm a lot more interested in you. If she got her feelings hurt, that's too bad. Don't hate the player, hate the game."

"Why would you be more interested in me?" I crossed my arms over my chest, my clutch still in my fingertips. "She was rubbing your dick and whispering dirty shit in your ear. She was a slam dunk."

"I don't need a slam dunk. My life is a fucking slam dunk."

"Wow...conceited much?"

"I'm blunt." He stepped closer to me, his hands remaining in his pockets like restraints. "I'm more interested in you because you're the most beautiful woman I've ever seen. When I saw you four years ago, I thought the same thing. I knew you would grow into your features, become a confident and sexy woman who owns the streets she struts down. Now, here you are...and I want you."

All I had to do was say yes. I could be naked in his bed in minutes. My legs could be wrapped around his waist, and I could lick the sweat off his chest. I wanted him four years ago, and I still wanted him now. "It's not going to happen, Hades."

His head tilted slightly, like my words were nonsense.

"We're associates. I'm not entirely sure what you do for Gustavo, but one day, you and I will be working together. I don't shit where I eat."

He continued to stare at me, as if he didn't hear a word I said. "You'll change your mind."

"I highly doubt it." Even if he didn't work with my family, he seemed like bad news. He seemed like a man that would capture my soul and shatter it. He was the kind of man that would ruin all other men. He would be fun for just a night, but anything more would be detrimental to my health.

He stepped closer to me, bringing our faces so near to each other that his breath fell across my skin. He kept his eyes focused on mine, his scent surrounding me like a blanket. When I didn't inch back, he moved farther in and placed his forehead against mine.

I should leave.

But I stayed.

He turned his head slightly, his eyes still on mine, and then he leaned in and kissed me. It was a soft contact between our lips, two pillows touching on a bed. When he moved his mouth, I could feel the coarse touch of his facial hair, the way it tickled me as it scraped against my skin. The kiss was innocent, slow and tender like our mouths were getting to know each other. He felt my lips with purpose, sucked on my bottom lip softly before he released it. Then he felt me again, filling me with his sexy, warm breath. His hands remained in his pockets just to prove a point.

All I had to do was pull away, but I couldn't. A simple kiss from him was intoxicating, addicting. It was so slow and gentle, nothing like our last embrace. He slowed down like we had all the time in the world to treasure it.

My hand slid up his forearm and touched the bicep in his thick arm. I kept going until I felt his chest, felt my fingers dig into his shirt the way that other woman had. Now I didn't care if he was rude when he ditched her for me. All I cared about was having him for myself. His kiss was better than sex, and if he was this good at kissing...imagine how good he was at fucking.

He pulled back, taking his delicious lips away from mine. Gloat was in his eyes as he looked at me, like he'd proved the point he wanted to make—a million times over. He held my gaze for a few more seconds, letting the desire dissolve into my blood. "You'll change your mind."

4

SOFIA

Gustavo and I took our seats at the long table, which was full of the members of the board. I hadn't realized we had a board of directors for our hotel, but my stepfather explained they had invested huge sums of money to get this place to open.

I took a seat, prepared to learn as much as possible. I had my pen and notebook out, ready to listen to what these men prioritized, how we intended to grow our brand awareness, how we could keep profits high and expenses low. Learning the trade was essential to growing it.

Gustavo began the meeting. "Let's start with the quarterly numbers." He nodded to me.

I stood up and distributed the packets to everyone.

"You gentlemen may not recognize her because she's all grown up, but this is Sofia." My stepfather said it proudly, as if I was his own daughter.

Most of the men didn't care. Some gave me a nod, while others ignored the information altogether.

I guess they'd already forgotten about my father.

Just when I sat down, the man to my right snapped his fingers. "Sweetheart, get me a coffee. No creamer but two sugars."

"I'll take the same," another asked. "And a banana muffin."

I stared at the first man in surprise, processing the request with confusion. I wasn't some assistant. I was the heir to the Tuscan Rose, the person aspiring to run this place in a few short years. I wasn't a coffee girl. "That's not in my job description, Marcus."

Gustavo shot me a look. "Just do it, Sofia. You said you wanted to contribute—that's how you contribute."

I wasn't above waiting on people. I worked as a waitress in college to pay my bills so I wouldn't have to take money from my mother. It just offended me that they would treat me so poorly, when I would own this place once my mother was gone. I rose to my feet and swallowed my pride. "Does anyone else want anything?"

THERE WAS a vacant office in the hallway, so I decided to claim it as mine. I had a laptop and a stack of papers, reading through material and organizing all of Gustavo's documents. While I sorted through the bookkeeping to get our taxes together, I noticed a discrepancy that didn't make any sense. When the number of bookings at the hotel were low, revenue stayed the same. On top of that, our private conference rooms were booked for several nights, but there was never any income from it.

Gustavo stepped inside. "Mr. Lombardi will be here in a few minutes. We'll be in the conference room for the next hour."

I set down the document I was reading. "Who's Mr. Lombardi?"

"You might know him as Hades."

Shit. I knew I would have to face him again eventually, but I thought it would take longer than a week. "Can I sit in?" I wasn't going to let his presence make me shy away from learning about that aspect of the company.

"No. I think it's best if you sit this out."

Gustavo was transparent about everything else, handing over his email account and all his documents, but for whatever reason, he continued to keep his conversations with Hades private.

It seemed like Hades was my best option for answers.

"While you're here, I actually have a question." I turned the documents around so he could view the highlighted portions. "There are some discrepancies in the reports. There are large deposits of cash that don't match room bookings, and there are also conference room rentals without any fees. I see it often, at least every month."

Gustavo didn't even bother to look at the paperwork. Instead of being interested in my report, he seemed more annoyed that I'd brought it up at all. "Leave it on my desk, and I'll look at it later. I need to get going."

THE ODD CONVERSATION with my stepfather worried me. He seemed like a good man who would never betray my mother, and if he did have his own agenda, he never would have allowed me to work with him every day. Obviously, I would catch him, figure out any wrongdoing. Money always left a paper trail.

Unless he thought I was too stupid to follow it.

I found that unlikely, but still I couldn't explain what I was looking at. I couldn't ask my mother about it because then I wouldn't be allowed to work with Gustavo at all. She would tell me to keep my mouth shut and find a husband instead.

She was a real piece of work.

I worked as a concierge that night, standing at the front desk and taking phone calls from guests who wanted to book activities when they came to visit. The rest of the time, I stood in the quiet lobby, thinking about my last conversation with Hades.

He said I would change my mind.

But he hadn't tried to make that happen.

Did I want him to make that happen?

My eyes were downcast as I looked at my computer, typing an email to a guest who wanted to inquire about dinner reservations at our Michelin star restaurant within the hotel. I gave them a list of available times then hit send.

When I lifted my gaze, he was standing there.

Hades Lombardi.

With brown eyes, dark hair, and beautiful Tuscan skin, he looked at me with the same hostility as before. It was a penetrating stare, as if he read my thoughts like words on paper. He was dressed in a black suit and tie even though it was unlikely he was working this late at night.

He'd caught me off guard, so I didn't know what to say.

I maintained a calm expression, borderline indifferent, and held his gaze. I tried not to think about our kiss on the side-walk in the dark, the way I felt his hard chest and wished he would grab me and pin me against the wall. Now I'd kissed him twice...and each embrace got better and better.

He pulled his hand out of his pocket and set a keycard on the counter.

I didn't glance at it, but I recognized it. It looked just like the keys we used at the hotel.

"Room 402." He held my gaze for a few more seconds before he walked to the elevators and stepped inside.

When the doors were shut, I stared at the card he'd left behind, the key he wanted me to have. The other reception-ists didn't seem to notice, so I dragged it off the counter and slipped it into my pocket.

My eyes returned to my computer screen so I could pretend I was working, but all I could think about was what was waiting for me in room 402. It was one of our deluxe suites, so it had a nice view, a large tub...and a king-size bed.

I shouldn't go. I should clock out and just go home.

But I knew that wasn't going to happen.

THE ELEVATOR TOOK me to the fourth floor.

I stepped into the deserted hallway, thankful I wouldn't have to see someone who might recognize me. Even if they did, they couldn't report me to anyone. One day, I might be their boss, so it would be stupid to piss me off.

I reached the door. The room number was in gold letters.

I stared at it with the key in my pocket, still considering my other option—take off and run. The key was grasped in my fingertips, and all I had to do was slide it through. But then Hades would have all the power. He would know he was the sexy bastard he claimed to be.

But fighting this feeling was getting me nowhere.

I unlocked the door and stepped inside.

Standing in front of the open window was Hades. Shirtless. His belt was pulled out of his slacks, so the pants hung low on his hips. The dramatic V-line was noticeable over his hips, even from where I stood several feet away. His side profile was visible, and he continued to stare at the city even when he heard the door.

The muscles of his sides were tight, chiseled, and defined. They wrapped all the way around until the muscles of his back were visible, bulging with strength. I'd never seen him shirtless, but I'd imagined it a couple of times.

I walked into the room, my heels lightly tapping against the carpet. I tossed my purse on the nearby table and stood there, waiting for him to address me. On the table was a bottle of scotch and two glasses. There was a golden-colored residue on the bottom of one, so he'd obviously started without me.

I stood behind him and examined his reflection in the glass. His eyes took in the scenery in front of him with a relaxed expression, but his jaw was slightly tight, like he was thinking about something.

I crossed my arms over my chest. "What exactly do you do for Gustavo—"

"You aren't here to talk." He turned around and faced me. With his bare feet, he walked across the carpet toward me, unbuttoning his slacks as he went. They came loose and slowly slid down his body, his black boxers emerging. "Neither am I. So let's just fuck." He pushed his boxers over his hips and let an impressive dick emerge. It was at half-mast, but even then, it was still something to show off.

I didn't take my clothes off as an act of defiance, but that wouldn't last long. I'd lost all power the second I'd stepped into his hotel room. He knew I wanted him, so there was no point in hiding it. There was also no point in keeping my clothes on when I could just walk out the door to demonstrate my independence.

"Take off your clothes." He kicked his pants and boxers away, standing there proudly with that big dick and ripped physique.

The longer I looked at his naked body, the less I cared about how stupid this was. The less I cared about the consequences. Maybe this would be a one-night stand, a good memory I could use with my vibrator in the future. Maybe there was no point in overthinking it. I unzipped the back of my skirt and let it fall over my hips until it hit the ground.

His gaze immediately dropped to my thong.

I unbuttoned my collared shirt and stripped it away. Underneath was a white cotton bra, not the sexiest piece of underwear I owned, but then again, I hadn't expected an erotic night like this. I peeled it off and let it fall into our pile of mutual clothes.

Hades looked me over, slowly walking toward me as he cherished the sight of my body. He took in my curves, my small nipples, my belly button. He saw everything. When his lips were close to mine, his arms wrapped around my waist and he pulled me into him, making my stomach press against his hard dick.

My god, it was big.

His hand slid into my hair, and he looked at me for a moment, treasuring the heat before the explosion. He fisted my strands and got a good grasp before he leaned in and kissed me, finishing the kiss we'd started last week.

When the desire started to burn my lips, I relaxed my body, and my brain turned off. My hands glided up his powerful back to the enormous shoulders I'd admired on so many occasions. My nails tested his neck, pressing deep into the surface to see if the skin would puncture.

His large hands moved to my ass and squeezed both cheeks as he kissed me, as he made love to my mouth with his. The kiss was so slow and tight, not sloppy and rushed like it was with inexperienced men. Every embrace was purposeful, deep. Sometimes there was tongue, but there was never saliva. Sometimes there was a deep breath, a masculine moan. Sometimes he could feel my lips tremble with desire, and he gave me a moment to catch my breath.

He touched me the way a man had never touched me before, his large hands squeezing me everywhere. My ass cheeks were practically bruised under his fingertips. My tits were handled like water balloons. He didn't treat me like a delicate woman who needed a soft touch. He touched me like I could handle it, could handle everything he was about to give me.

He guided me backward onto the bed, and we rolled together, the back of my head hitting the pillow. He pulled a condom from somewhere and slipped it on before he parted my legs with his knees, bringing us close together. His face rested over mine, and his arms pinned behind my knees as he sank inside me, his big dick stretching my little pussy.

He moaned against my lips, like he could feel just how tight I was. He sank deeper and deeper, stopping when his balls tapped against my ass. Now he breathed into my mouth, enjoying the way our bodies fit together like lock and key.

I felt the stretch of my body, felt my pussy ache from his intrusive presence. I'd never been with a man so big, who pushed in so deep. I was moaning against his mouth because I felt two things at once—pleasure and pain.

He started to rock into me, our breaths in sync.

"Fuck..." My fingers dug into his hair as I cradled his face close to mine. Our noses touched as we breathed together, my slickness oozing down my crack and onto the bedding underneath us. This was what I'd been craving for weeks, a big man to press me into the bed and fuck me good.

He thrust at a regular pace, making the headboard tap against the wall at a steady beat. It was the perfect speed, a rate that allowed me to enjoy every single thrust, treasure his tip to his base. I felt him completely fill me every time, his rock-hard dick pressing against every wall in my channel.

It was fucking incredible. "Yes...yes." I was just one of many, another notch on his bedpost, but I couldn't care less. I was honored to be there, honored to be fucked so good that night. "Don't stop." My hands moved up his chest, and I bit my bottom lip as I felt the climax approach, felt the heat numbing my fingertips.

He shifted his body closer to mine and fucked me harder, fucked me at a deeper angle.

"God..." I buried my face in his neck and released, my cunt squeezing his dick with the strength of a machine. I sheathed him with more slickness that traveled between my cheeks and to the sheets beneath me. It was so good, just to lie there and enjoy this sexy man fucking me.

He grabbed my hair and pulled me back to the pillow so he could look at me, could see the satisfaction in my eyes from the climax he'd just given me. "We aren't done yet."

His muscular arm was wrapped around my chest, his hand squeezing my tits as he fucked me from behind. We were spooning on our sides, his hips thrusting so he could get his dick as deep as possible. His lips rested against my ear, and I got to listen to his sexy breathing as he fucked me, as he enjoyed me.

I bounced my ass back against him, taking that girth with the same enthusiasm he gave it to me.

He held his weight on one elbow and leaned over me, supporting the back of my head as he turned my face toward his. Our lips came together, and he kissed me as he continued to pound into me.

My hand reached for the back of his neck, and I held on to him as we kissed, as we moved together, our bodies slick with my come. Hades ignited dreams I forgot I had, dreams of having a passionate affair that made me forget about everything happening outside those four walls. He was the lover I'd been waiting for, someone to waste my time until I had to grow up and make better choices. He was a mistake... but such a good one.

His lips hesitated as he came, filled another condom while being deep inside me. He grabbed on to my hip as he finished, giving me his entire length as he stuffed the tip of the latex. He closed his eyes for a second as he enjoyed the high before he rolled away and cleaned himself up.

I lay there, my body more satisfied than it'd ever been. All the guys I'd been with before were just practice.

This was actual fucking.

I could lie there and go straight to sleep.

I turned to the nightstand and noticed the time.

Shit, I had to get home.

I got out of bed and got dressed, doing my best to smooth the bird's nest on my head. I looked in the mirror on the wall and fixed my smeared mascara and reapplied a coat of lipstick from the tube in my purse. Even then, I still looked like I'd been thoroughly fucked. Hades had taken me over and over again, ready to start up again just minutes after the last go.

He returned to the bedroom, over six feet of masculine nakedness. Even when he wasn't hard, he still had a nice dick to show off, the kind that was big even when it was soft. He sauntered inside, carrying himself like a knight. He grabbed his boxers off the floor and pulled them up his muscular legs. "I can take you home."

And have my mother see? That was a crazy idea. "I don't mind walking."

"It's midnight."

"I like walking in the dark."

He rose to his feet and gave me a cold look. "That's too damn bad."

"Then I'll take a cab." My mother didn't care about the guys I ran around with, but she would definitely care if Hades Lombardi was the man I was sleeping with.

He pulled on his slacks then came toward me, so sexy that I wanted to jump into bed all over again. He looked me over, like a part of him still wanted more. The backs of his fingers reached my cheek and gently tucked my hair behind my ear.

When I'd walked into this room, I just wanted one night. I wanted to get his toxicity out of my system so I could move on with my life. But now that I'd had him, I was addicted. If sex was always like that, then why would I go anywhere else? "Give me your number."

That charming smile moved onto his lips, the affection

reaching his eyes. He tilted his head slightly as he looked at me. "Want to see me again?"

"I want to fuck you again."

His smile faded, and his eyes dropped their playfulness. He grabbed the phone out of my hand and typed in his number before he handed it back. "At your service."

"Good. Do you book your room under an alias?"

"I don't need to."

"My stepfather might wonder..."

"He won't wonder anything."

I didn't argue. "See you soon." I was tempted to kiss him goodbye, but to keep this casual, I didn't. I turned around to walk out.

"Sofia."

I turned around before I reached the door.

"This is all you want, right?" He stood with perfect posture, his shoulders back and his muscular arms tight. He was tanned everywhere, like he lay in the sun naked on a regular basis.

He probably wanted something casual, because he picked up women in bars and did whatever the fuck he wanted. Women probably wanted more from him, fell in love with him when they promised they wouldn't.

I wasn't one of those girls. "Nothing else."

5

HADES

THE CONFERENCE ROOM WAS FILLED WITH MY ASSOCIATES. ALL dressed in suits to blend in with the rest of the clientele of the hotel, they looked like royalty instead of the scumbags they really were.

Conversations filled the air, talking about money or pussy. Usually both. When I walked in, they all took notice of my presence, and as a sign of respect, they shut the fuck up. All the men relaxed in their chairs and turned to me.

I buttoned the front of my suit jacket as I stood at the head of the table. I surveyed all of them, holding back my rage because someone in that room was a traitor, a fucking rat that stepped out of line.

They would pay by the end of the night.

I snapped my fingers and turned to the doorway.

Maximum and Diesel pushed a cart into the room and closed the doors behind them as they left. Then they stood on guard, their guns concealed under their jackets just in case an employee happened to be in the wrong place at the wrong time.

I opened the container and pulled out a plastic bag. White crystals were inside, looking like small pieces of glass from a broken pitcher. I tossed it on the table, making all the men crane their necks to take a peek. "How many kilos do you think that is?"

No one was stupid enough to answer.

My hands slid into my pockets, and I walked around the table, passing behind the men like a really fucked-up game of duck, duck, goose. "It's five kilos. And at eight thousand euros per kilo...you can do the math. My chemists work in the best labs money can buy. Products aren't spilled. The yield is always the same. So, if someone skims cash off the top, I'll know about it." I kept moving, not looking any of them in the eye. If I made eye contact with the man who crossed me, I'd probably rip out his throat then and there. "Gentlemen, I've got eyes everywhere. My birds fly all the way to Russia, to Africa, to anywhere on this fucking planet. So if my shit is sold, I know about it. And I know exactly how much it's selling for. Do you know how much that is?"

The men glanced at each other, quickly figuring out that someone did something wrong.

"Eight thousand euros a kilo." I came full circle back to the front of the table. "But someone here is selling it at a higher price. And you know what they say...more money, more problems. That's only true if you aren't me. That money isn't coming back to me. I'm getting exactly the same amount as always. So...where did that money go?" I stopped when my eyes settled on Holton, the distributor working in Russia.

Our eyes locked for just seconds before the panic set in. "I don't know what you've heard—"

"Shut up."

He rose to his feet. "Hades, my guys are selling it at the right price. If they aren't, I can't control what they do."

"Really? Because when I tortured them, they said you raised the price."

Holton was shocked by this knowledge because he was stupid. How could he possibly think this shit would go unnoticed? Just because we worked thousands of miles apart didn't mean I didn't know exactly where he took a shit every day.

Holton glanced around the room, looking for an escape route.

"You want to leave?" I asked.

He stayed silent, knowing it was a trick question.

I nodded to my guys.

"No!" Holton tried to run around the table, but Maximum blocked him in. Diesel went the other way, cornering him like a scared dog. The remaining associates in their chairs didn't look up from the table, pretending to ignore what was happening right before them.

"Hades, I'm sorry." Holton turned to me, letting Maximum grab him and drag him away. "Please, I have a daughter. I'll pay you every cent that I owe you, alright? Please." Maximum dragged him to one of the large windows that was twelve stories above the sidewalk. Diesel unlocked it and pushed it open.

When Holton realized what was happening, he screamed. "Hades, don't do this."

"You've already paid me back, Holton. I saw to that." I sauntered toward him, my hands resting in my pockets.

Knowing the ground had been pulled from underneath his feet, Holton's eyes shone with a gloss, probably from the harshness of the wind that was blowing into the room. "My family... Please don't hurt my family."

I'd never been interested in torturing innocents. But of course, I never told anyone that. "If you don't want me to hurt them, you'll keep your mouth shut and not say a word all the way down."

His mouth opened then his bottom lip trembled. "All the way down...?"

Maximum pulled him to the ledge.

"Hades, come on." He tried to squirm out of his hold, but Maximum was far too big to be pushed away.

"Make a sound, and they all die."

When Holton understood this was the end, there was such defeat in his eyes. He would have screamed like all other cowards, but knowing his family was on the line silenced him. Nothing he said could change my mind—and he knew that.

I just wanted him to shut up so we didn't attract any unwanted attention. We'd booked a hotel room for him a few floors down. Everyone would think he'd jumped himself, that it was a sad story of suicide.

I nodded to Maximum. "Do it."

Holton clenched his jaw tighter to control his screams. He grunted as he tried to fight back, as he tried to hold on to something as he was shoved out the window. He held on to the windowsill with a few fingers, desperate to survive.

Maximum kicked him and down he went.

We were so high up, we didn't hear his body collide with the ground, only the shriek of a woman down below.

I turned back to the table. "Did you hear that, gentlemen? Silence."

"So you pushed him out a fucking window?" Damien sat across from me at the dining table in my four-story home in the heart of Florence. I had a secure parking garage and a large fence around my property for privacy. There was decent land for trees and an outdoor pool, but for the most part, I spent my time indoors. I had an entire block to myself —and no neighbors were the best kind of neighbors. "I didn't push him. Maximum did."

"But still—hard-core."

"He raised the price of my product and pocketed the profit. That's stealing."

"True..."

"People who steal from me never live long."

"Double true." He puffed on his cigar and let the smoke rise to the ceiling.

We shared a bottle of scotch, just the way we used to when

we were young. Now we were almost thirty...but we hadn't slowed down a bit. I liked smelling cigars more than smoking them, but when Damien lit up, I couldn't resist the urge.

"So, everything taken care of?"

"Always."

"If you raised the profits of that shipment and people were paying, maybe you could do the same with the rest."

"We're always laundering so much."

"So?" He shrugged. "The government can't be that dumb. They just look the other way because they don't want to get pushed out a window."

I grinned slightly. "You know I don't mess with the police."

"Because you've never had to. If push came to shove—"

"Everyone has a price. I'll just pay them off."

"Pretty soon we'll have to pay off everyone in Italy."

I shrugged. "So be it." Damien and I had founded our bank years ago, with the sole intention of laundering money from our drug enterprise. But as the years passed, more men wanted a piece of the pie—including the Tuscan Rose. Sofia had no idea Gustavo was laundering the money I gave him for offering a neutral place for meetings. I'd done more deals at the Tuscan Rose than anywhere else.

I felt bad for the girl... She'd be devastated when she found out.

"When is the money coming in?" Damien asked. "I just

asked our guys about the ship in the Mediterranean, but the winds have been unkind."

My phone vibrated in my pocket, so I pulled it out to check the message.

It was from Sofia. *I get off work in twenty minutes.*

It was impossible not to grin at that message.

"What the fuck are you smiling about over there?" Damien relaxed in his chair and put his feet on the table. "You only smile for money or pussy. Which one is it?"

"The second one."

"You can always have too much money, but never too much pussy. Who's the girl?"

Damien had been my friend for more than ten years. There were no secrets between us. But I wouldn't betray Sofia's identity, and I wouldn't describe her fuckable tits and her even more fuckable ass. Her secrets were safe with me. "Nobody."

MY FINGERS SPANNED her entire back, my thumbs touching across her belly. I guided her up and down, feeling her hips undulate as she ground her clit against my hard body, pleasing herself without shame. Every time she rolled her hips, she arched her back in the sexiest way, pressed her tits farther into my face.

Damn, whores didn't even fuck this good.

I leaned against the headboard and watched her fuck me,

felt her airtight pussy slide up and down my dick, slathering it with another layer of cream. Every time she lifted her body, I could see the cream build up around the base of my dick.

Her tits were so damn amazing. They were small, with little nipples, but they fit her petite size so well. I liked to watch them shake up and down as she worked up a sweat fucking me. Last time we'd met in this hotel room, she'd lain there while I'd fucked her brains out.

Now it was her turn.

My hands cupped her tits and squeezed them like stress balls while my cock twitched with joy. Nothing better than being balls deep in a beautiful woman with my hands full of tits.

She bounced on my dick harder and harder, using my shoulders as an anchor as she really got herself going. She arched her back deeply every time, her ass looking amazing in the mirror on the wall. Her whimpers became higher in pitch, and she started biting her bottom lip in preparation for another climax.

She pressed her face against mine as she came, moaning and clawing me at the same time.

I spanked her ass. "Come, baby."

She moaned.

I spanked her again. "Come all over this dick."

Her nails dragged down my chest as she finished, yelling, screaming, and whimpering all at the same time. "God..." Her hand dug deep into her hair as she finished, as if she didn't know how else to process the pleasure. "I love your dick."

My cock twitched inside her, pleased with her compliment. I grabbed her hips and pulled her down onto me a couple of times until I hit my threshold. Then my toes curled and my fingers dug into her skin as I came, my hips thrusting involuntarily as I finished shooting my load into the condom.

My head rested against the headboard as I stared at her, my chest rising and falling rapidly as my body returned to normal. My fingers loosened their hold, and I stared at her messy hair, her beautiful green eyes. She had thick brown hair, dark in color and so exotic. It was soft to the touch, shiny under the light. I'd been with so many beautiful women in so many places, but this woman had a special quality. It wasn't just her perfect body, her doll-like face, or her full lips. It was something else...something I noticed the moment I laid eyes on her.

When I said she was the most beautiful woman I'd ever seen...I meant it.

My hand snaked into her hair and pulled it from her cheek as I cradled her close to me. My dick had softened inside her, but I wasn't eager to break free. My thumb brushed across her bottom lip, feeling the smoothness and the wetness of my own saliva. I'd already fucked her twice, but I still wanted more...I wanted her.

I pulled her into me and kissed her.

She kissed me back, still out of breath from fucking me like she was paid to do it.

My fingers continued to stroke her hair, feel the quickening pulse in her neck. I touched her small tongue with my own, felt her racing heartbeat against my palm. I scooted her closer to me and deepened the kiss, falling into the bliss this woman gave me. It wasn't just good sex. It was passionate, satisfying, dreamlike. A fuck with a woman was usually a one-time thing, and even if it wasn't, I didn't necessarily look forward to the next one. But with Sofia, I already couldn't wait until the next time I saw her.

She had been just eighteen years old when I first wanted to fuck her. If she had been older, I would have lifted up her dress and fucked her against the wall outside the party. But she was too young, too innocent. I was an asshole to the worst degree...but I wouldn't do something like that. We were still the same number of years apart, but now she was a grown woman, a woman with confidence and experience.

Judging from the way she fucked me, she knew exactly what she was doing.

Her hands glided up my chest, and she kissed me like she never wanted it to end. When she'd looked at me in the bar, her gaze had been full of dislike. But now she touched me like she couldn't live without me, like I was her reason to keep breathing.

After a few minutes of heated kisses, she pulled away and ran her fingers through her hair. Her eyes glanced at the clock sitting on the nightstand and checked the time. "It's getting late..." She tried to move off me.

"No." I grabbed her by the elbow and pulled her back on top of me. "I'm not done."

"It's almost eleven."

"And when it's midnight, it'll be just as late." My hand glided into her hair once more, pulling it from her beautiful face. Her makeup had been washed away by the sweat, but that somehow made her more stunning. She looked like a woman who had just been fucked, and since I'd done the fucking, it was a turn-on.

"What kind of batteries do you run on?" she asked, her fingertips lightly stroking my chest. She referred to my sexual prowess, my surprising endurance.

"You."

She tilted her head slightly.

"If I were that horny all the time, I would never leave the house. You make me this way." I didn't want her to get off my lap, to take away that sexy ass and those gorgeous tits. I wished I could come home to her open legs every night, just slide between her thighs and fuck her before I went to sleep.

"You make me this way too..." Her eyes dropped so she could watch her hands. She still possessed a hint of shyness, a small resemblance to the girl I'd met on the balcony. She'd grown into a confident woman since then, but it was nice to see the vulnerable side of her once in a while.

"Then we should do this more often."

"I wish...but we can't get caught."

Gustavo wouldn't be pleased to know I was fucking his step-daughter, but because of our business arrangement, he wouldn't do anything about it. I didn't care if her mother knew about it. But I suspected Sofia would be embarrassed if her family had any information about her personal life, and if she knew I was a drug dealer, she would probably be disturbed by that...even though her family members were also criminals. "It makes it more fun that way."

She gently moved off me, letting my dick and the condom slide out of her. She rolled to my side and lay down, her perfect body on display for me to enjoy.

I grabbed a handful of tissues and cleaned off before I lay flat on my back.

She stared at me. "How do you feel about cuddling?"

I patted my chest.

She smiled and moved into me, inserting her leg between my knees while resting her head on my shoulder. Her arm draped over my waist, her fingertips slightly exploring the grooves of muscle of my physique. "So...what do you with Gustavo?"

I knew the question would come up. It was also obvious that Gustavo wasn't giving her any information. I gave her the truth but left out all the good stuff. "I'm his banker."

"His personal banker?"

"No. For the Tuscan Rose. He uses my bank for the hotel's finances, and I help manage his payments and assets. He has a hefty loan from me, and I invest his profits to pay off the loan quicker." The specifics didn't matter. When her family was ready to come clean, she would know then. It wasn't my place to get involved.

She accepted the information without prying further. Her fingers continued to explore my body, and her body softened as she relaxed into me. Her curves were so perfect, her sexy hips and her tiny little waist. Her straight brown hair was exquisite, so nice to fist when I wanted to anchor her in place. Her bottom lip was shaped like a bow, and it was as plump as a cherry, full of juice I wanted to suck dry.

Fucking beautiful.

She could be a damn model if she wanted, command a ridiculous salary to be on billboards all over the world. She could be the highest-paid courtesan in Europe, gaining millions of euros for just a single night of her time.

But instead, she wanted to manage a hotel.

I respected her for it.

She sat up and tucked her hair behind her ear, the rest falling across my chest as she moved. "Thanks for tonight..." She rose to her feet and fetched her clothes. Her bra had landed on the back of the chair, hanging by a single hook.

I stared at her ass as she walked away, mesmerized by the subtle shake back and forth. Her movements were primal, and she turned me into an animal just by watching her. I wanted to pin her to the ground and claim her as mine.

She started to get dressed, keeping her back turned to me. She clasped her bra around her waist, and she pulled her black dress over her perfect body. Watching her put her clothes on was somehow just as sexy as when she took them off.

The other women I'd been with were all the same. They were attracted to my wealth, my power. They got off on the way I bossed everyone around. They even got off on the times I murdered my enemies. Once, I shot a man right between the eyes, and a woman sucked my dick immedi-ately afterward. And they always wanted more...something I couldn't give. Flings didn't last long because they blossomed into conversations about the future. That was why I hardly ever saw the same woman twice.

But Sofia seemed to want nothing to do with me.

Maybe it was because our worlds were intertwined and it wasn't professional. But I suspected she had stronger reasons for crossing me off her list. Her mind and body were at war with each other. When her body was being satisfied, she ignored all the logic her brain tried to give her. She liked fucking in a hotel room because it was so meaningless—like it was an affair.

I got out of bed and pulled on my boxers. Her back was turned to me, so I approached her slowly, my eyes examining the nape of her neck. Her hair was pulled over one shoulder, and she bent down to slip her heels on.

When she stood upright, my arms circled her waist, and I pulled her close to me, my lips immediately tasting the delicate skin of her neck.

She immediately turned her face away, exposing herself to a deeper kiss.

My lips sucked that perfectly fair skin, making it flush the color of a pink rose petal. My arms tightened on her flat stomach, and I pulled her deep into me, my hands caressing her tits through her bra.

She didn't fight back. She let me have her...all of her.

I kissed her neck then rested my lips against her ear. "Sofia, you're an amazing woman."

She backed her ass into me, rubbing against my hard-on

through the cotton. "No, Hades. You're the one who's amazing…"

I closed my eyes as I squeezed her a little tighter, so hard I was going to rip through my boxers so I could get to that pussy. I'd just fucked this woman plenty of times, but now I bent her over the table and yanked her dress up over her ass.

She gripped the edge of the table and deepened the arch in her back, popping her ass up because she wanted it, because her pussy was still wet even though she'd had enough orgasms to last a week.

I rolled the condom onto my dick and slid inside her, listening to her breathe deeper as she took every inch.

Her hand moved to the back of my neck, and she positioned our faces so we could see each other, see the mutual look of desire we both possessed. "Fuck me, Hades. Fuck me hard."

Jesus. "Yes, baby."

6

SOFIA

I WALKED THROUGH THE FRONT DOOR AT ONE IN THE MORNING.

I locked the fourteen-foot double doors behind me and stepped into the grand entryway of my family home. With the thick walls and the structure surrounding our estate, it was easy to forget the city was right outside. All the noise from cars and passersby diminished once I was on the property—making me feel alone.

I began the long journey up the stairs, my feet dragging because I was exhausted from working all morning and all afternoon...and then fucking like crazy at night. Did I have any regrets? Hell no. But I was fucking tired.

My eyes were downcast, and I didn't notice my mother standing at the top of the stairs. In her loose nightgown with her hair pinned back and a green mask on her face, she looked like a demon.

Startled, I took a few steps back. "Shit. Don't creep up on people like that, Ma."

"I'm not creeping. I've been standing here the whole time, watching you do your walk of shame up the stairs."

I shouldered my purse and sighed, not wanting to conjure some false explanation for my whereabouts. My hair was messy despite my attempt to straighten it, and my lips were swollen because Hades couldn't stop kissing me. When my lips were exhausted, he moved elsewhere, making my nipples raw. "It's late. You should go to sleep."

"I was in the mood for a cookie, so I snuck into the kitchen and grabbed one."

"You don't eat cookies."

She shrugged. "I do when I can't sleep. Gustavo is snoring like an animal, so now I don't know what to do."

"We have guest rooms…"

"Yeah, but I hate sleeping alone."

I cocked an eyebrow. "You aren't sleeping with me."

She rolled her eyes. "You wish, darling."

"No, I don't. I don't want that green shit on my pillow."

"You're going to need to start doing this soon if you want to look young forever."

"I'm not even in my mid-twenties. I have some time."

She crossed her arms over her chest, her chin held high. "I started when I was twenty-one—so you're late."

I dismissed this conversation by turning around and walking to my room. "Goodnight, Ma."

"Goodnight, honey." Her voice followed me down the hallway. "Who's this man who is robbing you of all your sleep?"

I stopped in my tracks, not surprised she'd picked at the elephant in the room. I slowly turned back to her. "No one worth mentioning."

"He must be good. You spend a lot of time with him."

He was damn good—but I wouldn't say that to my mother. "Goodnight." I continued walking to my room.

"Enjoy it while you can, honey. Because one day you'll blink...and all the good times of your life will be behind you."

HADES and I were just having meaningless sex in a hotel room, so I could go out with whomever I wanted. But I didn't go on any dates or give any guy a chance. All I wanted was good sex that wasn't complicated, and since I had it, I didn't see the point in pursuing something else.

I wasn't looking for Mr. Right, so why bother?

There was no such thing as Mr. Right anyway.

I worked throughout the week, helping Gustavo run the company while dealing with the police that had come to investigate a suicide that had happened at our hotel. Apparently, some man jumped off his balcony and broke his skull when he hit the concrete. There was a brief suicide note. Seemed like he had money troubles. We managed to keep it quiet so it wouldn't stain the impeccable reputation of the Tuscan Rose.

I worked morning and nights, constantly on my feet and in heels all day. It took so much work to break through Gustavo's armor because he was only willing to give me a few responsibilities. I didn't touch the money, and he pulled me off bookkeeping...probably because I was asking too many questions.

Whenever I saw members of the board, they treated me with the same indifference. As if I were still the little girl I was when my father was alive, they treated me like someone who wasn't even old enough to drive. The only task I was qualified for was fetching coffee.

It was bullshit.

It would take time to sway their opinion, to earn their respect, and I was willing to wait as long as I had to for that to happen. This was my family's legacy, my father's lifetime achievement. It shouldn't belong to a group of old men who didn't care about anything besides money. It should belong to someone who cared about having fresh flowers in the lobby constantly, putting special treats in the rooms when guests were celebrating something special, accommodating couples for a table at the restaurant even when it was booked solid. That's what made this hotel great. It seemed like everyone in the back office lost sight of that, Gustavo included.

Gustavo had been coughing all day, making booming noises that announced all the shit caught in his throat. He sounded sicker than a dog, so sick that he should have been in bed days ago. But he was a workaholic and refused to leave, even if that meant making the rest of us sick.

Thankfully, I had a badass immune system.

Gustavo knocked on my door then quickly coughed into his elbow. His throat sounded so hoarse it seemed like he'd swallowed sandpaper. "I'm going to go home and rest."

About time. "Good. Drink lots of fluids."

"I have a meeting with Mr. Lombardi in a few minutes. I tried to cancel, but he's already at the hotel."

"I could handle it for you."

"I was actually going to ask if you could reschedule it."

I was not that incompetent. "Sure."

"I'll see you in a few days." He coughed again then walked out, wrapping his coat around him.

Fall was deepening, slowly beginning to resemble winter as months passed. The streets were becoming icy at night, and I'd started to bring a jacket to work to protect me from the cold as I walked home.

The thought of seeing Hades sent a short thrill down my spine, but that didn't last long. He wasn't coming here as my lover, as the man who gave me the best sex I'd ever had. He was just a business associate, someone who wasn't important. I controlled my reaction within seconds and reminded myself I wasn't about to get laid.

That would have to wait until tonight.

A minute later, Hades appeared in my doorway. Today, he'd ditched the suit and wore dark jeans and a long-sleeved green shirt. The fabric was tight on his muscular arms, snug on his powerful chest, and highlighted his slender waist and hips. He looked delicious in a suit, but he somehow looked better in this casual look.

He didn't smile when he looked at me, but his eyes greeted me in their own way. They were his bedroom eyes, the same look he gave me when I was naked underneath him, my wet cunt taking his fat dick over and over.

I refused to think about that. "Gustavo is sick, but I'm sure I can help you with whatever needs to be taken care of."

He sauntered farther into my office then shut the door behind him.

"You can leave it open."

He ignored my request and sat in the chair opposite me. "I prefer it closed." He crossed one leg, his ankle resting on the opposite knee. His hands came together in his lap, and his large frame hid the chair from view. His eyes took a quick glance at my office before they settled on me again. Once they were there, they didn't move.

I didn't waste my time arguing with him. "Gustavo didn't have time to give me instructions. He was feeling so unwell that he needed to leave immediately. If you could tell me what needs to be done, I could assist you." I sat perfectly upright in my hair, my hands together on the desk like he was any other faceless client.

Hades stared at me like he hadn't listened to a word I said.

I stayed quiet, hoping he would say something helpful.

"Do you collect the money? Because I think most of our profits are immediately wired to the bank from our customers."

"It's more than that. I organize all of Gustavo's expense reports, keeping everything organized so he has an exact understanding of cash flow. Maybe in time, you'll be able to give that to me, but for now, I think it's best if I get that information from him." He pushed me to the sidelines, just the way everyone else did.

I tried not to be offended by it. He shouldn't give me special treatment just because he was fucking me. "Then there's nothing more for us to talk about." I rose to my feet. "I'll walk you out."

"Sit." He made his command from his seated position, not raising his voice to get my attention. His voice was so naturally deep that it took almost no effort to be taken seriously.

I continued to stand out of defiance.

He smiled slightly, like he was amused by my rebellion. "Have dinner with me tonight."

I slowly lowered my body into my chair, surprised he would ask such a thing. "I'm busy."

"With?"

"Does it matter?" I didn't owe him an explanation. I didn't ask for anything more than his dick.

His eyes narrowed. "You aren't working tonight at the hotel. So, what are you doing that's so important you can't have dinner with me?"

My eyes widened. "Excuse me? How do you know when I'm working?"

"Because I know more about this hotel than you do."

That was an insult I didn't appreciate. "I don't see the necessity in having dinner. I'd rather just get right to the good stuff." This man made me feel the extreme version of every emotion. When I came, I came hard. When I felt weak, it was like I couldn't stand. When I felt passion, I felt like I would die without him in my arms. When I was pissed...I was super pissed.

"Having a conversation with me would be that terrible?"

"No...but I'd rather not blur the lines."

"Meaning?"

This guy was a playboy, so he knew exactly what I meant. Only sex—no strings attached. "I just want to fuck you. I don't want anything else to do with you. It's pretty simple, so I don't know why you're making it complicated."

"I'm making it complicated?" he asked, slightly amused. "You're the one overreacting."

"I'm not overreacting. I'm just not interested in that kind of relationship with you."

"Really?" He cocked his head slightly, arrogantly. "Because when we're behind closed doors, you can't keep your hands off me."

"Two completely different things." I refused to be embarrassed by my attraction to him. When we were together, all my walls came down. I was just a woman in the throes of passion with the perfect man. I didn't think about anything else besides what we were doing, how he made me feel. Now, he was making me think...and it was exhausting.

"Have dinner with me." He returned to the same request, asking it calmly like he hadn't just asked me minutes ago. His elbows rested on the arms of his chair, and he brought his fingers together, looking at me like I might give a different answer.

"I said no." I rose to my feet again. "We don't sit around and talk. We don't share a bottle of wine on a date. We fuck —that's it."

"Who said it was a date?"

"Then what else is it?"

He shrugged. "We're going to be working together for a long time. Maybe we should get to know each other."

"If you meant that, you would show me exactly what documents you're looking for."

He held my gaze, his eyes hiding his thoughts so perfectly.

"Hades, let's get something straight." I slowly lowered myself back into the chair. "We meet in a hotel room a few nights a week. We don't need to make small talk. We don't even need to pretend to care about each other. It is what it is, and that's what makes it so good. So just leave it alone."

He relaxed against the back of the chair, his jaw slightly tight like he was taking my words with a grain of salt. "Alright."

Good. The argument was over.

"Some guy break your heart?"

"Excuse me?" I blurted, provoked by the blunt question.

"You're so cold, I had to ask."

"I'm not cold. Just not looking for a relationship."

"And why is that?" he asked, tilting his head to the side.

"Does it matter?"

"It matters to me."

I'd never had a guy drag this information out of me. All of my other flings were easy to walk away from. They happened, and when they were done, it was over. "I just don't want to be in a relationship. I like playing the field. I like seeing what's out there." Not that it was any of his business.

He looked confused, like he couldn't believe what I'd just said.

"I don't want to be tied to one man. I don't want to fall in love. I just want to focus on me."

He still looked perplexed. "I've never heard a woman say that before."

"I don't see why it's so hard to follow. Most men don't want to be in a relationship, and they give you the exact same response. But since I'm a woman, there must be something wrong with me. It's sexist and annoying."

His confusion disappeared. Now his expression was hard to read. He was just a beautiful man staring at me. "What about kids?"

"What about them?"

"You never want to have a family?"

"I never said I *never* wanted to get married. I'm just not interested in something serious right now. I'm only twenty-two and not in any hurry to settle down. I just want to have fun and not owe anyone an explanation. Don't expect me to apologize for being honest. So, if you're looking for something permanent or long-term, I'm not your girl."

"I can see that." He smiled slightly. My speech seemed to amuse him. Instead of taking it seriously and matching my somber mood, he found it comical, even though that wasn't my intention. "I'm not looking for that either. You and I have the same interests. That being said, I would love to take you to dinner. I would love to stare at you over candlelight, share a bottle of wine with you, and then fuck you exactly how you want me to."

Now that my desires were completely clear, I didn't see the harm in it. "Someone might see us together…"

"I don't give a fuck who sees us together. Gustavo needs me more than I need him, so if he has a problem with it, that's too damn bad."

"But it could make me look bad. The board already doesn't like me."

"That's your problem right there."

"Excuse me?" Sometimes he was calm, and sometimes he was aggressive. I never knew what he was going to hit me with.

"You care what other people think. People will respect you a lot more when you don't."

HADES and I sat at a table in the back, far away from the other guests enjoying their meals in the dim lighting, with the sounds of the Spanish guitar and the clanking of glasses as people made their private toasts. The place was fancier than I expected, so my dress felt a little casual.

He didn't seem to mind.

He ignored the menu in front of him and immediately ordered a bottle of wine for the table. Not once did he look at the waiter, and he didn't bother to at least say hello first. He barked out orders like a general rather than a paying customer.

"I'm not impressed by the way you treat people."

He stilled at my observation, subtly offended by what I said. "I know what I want, and I get to the point."

"But there are better ways of getting that across."

He held my gaze for nearly a minute as he formulated his response. "When you're in charge, you make decisions. People turn to you for direction, and you give it to them. That's the quality of a good leader."

"But you aren't the leader of this restaurant."

"Yes, I am. I own this place."

I picked up my menu, slightly blindsided by his admission. "Of course you do…"

The waiter returned with the uncorked bottle of wine and two glasses. Just when he turned to disappear, Hades spoke again. "Thank you, Hector."

Hector turned back to him, clearly surprised by what he'd said. It took him a second to respond. "You're welcome, sir." He disappeared.

I couldn't wipe off the smile on my face. "Wasn't so hard, huh?"

He drank his wine as he watched me, not interested in the menu still lying on the table.

I made my selection then set it down. "Already know what you want?"

"I always know what I want." He got the waiter's attention again by simply raising his hand a few inches off the table.

Hector returned and took our order.

Once he was gone, we stared at each other. He hardly blinked as he looked at me, as he took in my features while the candle burned low between us. His brown eyes were a little lighter in the glow, and his sharp features seemed a little softer in a different atmosphere.

"I knew this was a bad idea..."

"We've been here five minutes."

"Yeah. But I would much rather be naked with you right now."

His eyes narrowed at my confession, and his body tightened noticeably. His body was all muscle, concealed under his perfect skin. Whenever his core contracted, everything else moved with it. His fingertips rested on the stem of his glass, his body perfectly still as he internalized what I'd said. "I can fuck you here if you'd like."

"Right here on this table?" I asked incredulously.

"Like I said, I don't give a shit what people think."

Something told me he was being serious, even though the

room was full of people. I drank my glass and entertained myself with his handsome features, thinking about how we would fuck once we got to the hotel. I was in the mood for something deep and slow, like the first night we were together and he pressed me deep into the mattress. I wanted to treasure the feeling of his dick inside me, feel that amazing stretch.

But I had to get through this first. It was a dinner I didn't want to have, and I didn't have any interest in getting to know him when I already knew exactly what he was. He was a rich playboy who went from woman to woman. I just happened to be the flavor of the week, but when he saw the next beautiful woman, he would forget all about me. His text messages would stop, and there would be no more invitations to the hotel room.

I was dreading that moment.

I'd found the best sex of my life, and I wasn't willing to let it go so soon. Most guys I'd been with either didn't know what they were doing or they cared more about getting off than getting you off. Hades did neither of those things...and he was fucking gorgeous. Why would I want to ruin that by getting to know him? What little I knew about him, I didn't like, like when he dropped that pretty girl the instant he saw someone better. That was his entire life...moving from one chick to the next. He was a heartless asshole.

The less I knew, the better.

I swirled my wine and took another drink. "So...you're almost thirty." There wasn't much for us to talk about, so I pulled at whatever I could find.

He nodded slightly.

"Are you dreading the big three-oh?"

"Why would I be?"

"Because your youth is officially gone."

"Thirty isn't that old. I'm just getting started."

It wasn't that old, but he was seven years ahead of me, and that felt like a lifetime. He had nearly a decade of experience more than I did. That was probably why he knew exactly how to fuck a woman.

Knew exactly how to fuck me.

"Do you ever think of settling down?" I asked, pressing personal questions to him the way he did to me.

He gave a simple answer. "No."

"You don't want kids?"

"I do—someday."

"So, you do think about settling down?"

He shrugged. "Maybe when I meet the right woman, that'll be an option. But for the last ten years, it hasn't crossed my mind."

I nodded slightly. "My mother thinks I need to get married soon. Find a respectable husband who will take care of me." I rolled my eyes. "She thinks I should stay home all day and leave the business to the man."

He didn't tease me for the archaic viewpoint. "You have a wealthy family. It's not unheard of for people to protect their bloodlines."

"Please don't tell me you agree with her."

"I'm not exactly a romantic, so I don't think arranged marriages are so bad. Most marriages end in divorce because people choose wrong. They have no idea what to look for in a partner, what kind of relationship will last for fifty years. They think with their emotions rather than logic, so they marry for all the wrong reasons. By finding a suitable partner that checks off all the boxes, you eliminate all of that."

I swirled my glass of wine again and took a drink. "I don't have a problem with arranged marriages. I don't have a problem with regular marriages either. I just wish I had the option to never marry. Marriage seems to be a prerequisite in order for me to have any hold on our hotels...which shouldn't matter. My marital status shouldn't make me more or less qualified. It's sexist and idiotic. You run your own business. You aren't married."

"But I'm a man."

"And that's sexist," I snapped.

"It's not. Most men are assholes, and assholes only respect other assholes. Your mother's concern about your ability to run your line of hotels isn't unfounded. People will try to push you around, to make you so miserable that you quit in tears. Having a strong husband whom they fear will make your life a million times easier—even if he has nothing to do with the business. I'm not saying it's right. I'm not saying it's fair. But that's the world we live in." He drank from his glass then turned his head when he spotted someone he recognized. He straightened in his chair and set his glass to the side, a slight smile on his lips.

"They let you show your ugly face in here?" A tall man of similar age approached our table. With dark hair and a slimmer build, he was equally handsome, just in a different way. Behind him was a beautiful woman in a skintight purple dress, her hair done and earrings hanging from her lobes.

"Only to scare you off." Hades rose to his feet and greeted his friend with a quick hand grasp. It wasn't a formal handshake, just a gesture of affection between two guys. "Who's your lovely friend?"

He turned to the woman that must be his date. "Pritchet? Pruitt? I can't pronounce it."

The woman in purple shook his head. "Pruzovoski." She spoke with a Russian accent so thick, it seemed unlikely she spoke English.

"Pleased to meet you." Hades moved to my side of the table. "Sofia, this is my friend and business partner, Damien."

Damien took my hand, smiled, and then kissed the back of my wrist. "Pleasure to meet you." When he dropped my hand, he turned back to Hades. "Nobody, huh?"

Hades ignored his comment. "Would you guys like to join us?"

Was this a double date? Did that make it more or less formal?

"Yes." Damien pulled out the chair for his date. "As long as you're buying."

DAMIEN'S DATE couldn't say two words that we could understand, so she stayed quiet most of the night, feeding Damien pieces of bruschetta and anything else that was small enough to shove into his mouth. Once he finished chewing, she always kissed him like she wished they were somewhere private—without two people sitting across from them at the table.

Hades rested his arm over the back of my chair, his fingers lightly slipping into the back of my hair. Sometimes he would get a handful and give me a gentle tug, a preview of what he would do to me later when we got back to the hotel.

Damien turned to Hades, his girl all over him. "So, what's new?"

"I see you every day. There's never anything new." Hades was still the cold guy he was all the time, but he seemed to have a special softness for his friend. His tone was much less aggressive, and he was actually playful.

"Well, you didn't tell me about her." Damien nodded to me. "That's new."

"That's because there's nothing to say." His fingers moved under my hair and felt the skin of my neck. He grabbed on to me gently, holding me as his thumb brushed against the softness of my skin.

"You tell me about all your girls," Damien said. "The fact that you didn't tell me about her is new." He opened his mouth so his date could shove another appetizer into it. Another kiss ensued, where she whispered in Russian against his ear.

"Do you have any idea what she's saying?" Hades asked.

Damien shrugged. "No. I think that's why I like her."

Dinner was finished after an hour of talking, and since there was no tab to pay, we were free to go whenever we were ready.

I leaned into him, eager to get his clothes off so we could do what we did best. This dinner only proved to me that we had nothing in common, no connection. I knew he operated a bank and the hotel was one of his clients, but other than that, he was an enigma. According to Damien's comments, Hades was as much of a playboy as I assumed he was, having different women every time they spoke. That didn't make a difference to me, but that made me want to skip these dinners and get down to business. I kissed his neck then brought my lips to his ear. "Take me to the hotel and fuck me already."

He turned my way, slightly amused by my request. "Then let's go." He rose from the chair and grabbed my hand as he prepared to walk out. "I'll see you tomorrow, Damien. And lovely to meet you."

She smiled and waved to both of us.

He wrapped his arm around my waist and escorted me away from the table.

"I want all the details tomorrow, Hades," Damien called after him. "So be ready."

Hades kept walking and guided me outside. His car was parked at the curb, pitch-black with blacked-out windows.

"Didn't know guys gossiped so much."

He opened the passenger door for me. "I don't gossip about

you." He shut the door then got into the driver's seat beside me.

"You didn't tell him about the woman you're nailing at the Tuscan Rose?" I asked as I fastened my seat belt. "The girl that you ground up against when she was eighteen years old?" That sounded too juicy not to share.

"No." He pulled onto the street and drove.

"And why not?"

"I don't want to."

"It sounds like you tell him about all your other girls. Why not me?"

He kept his eyes on the road and let my question sit in the air. He ended the conversation completely when he turned on the radio and allowed the music to cover the tension his rejection created.

I let it go.

After a few blocks, he pulled up to a large building with enormous walls for privacy.

"Why are we here?"

"Because it's where I live."

I glanced at the fortress before I turned back to him. "I don't want to go to your place. I prefer the hotel."

"Well, we're already here." The steel gate opened, and he pulled his car inside.

"It takes five minutes to drive back to the hotel."

"This bed or that bed, what does it matter?" He parked in an underground garage and killed the engine.

"It matters because the hotel is walking distance to my place."

He gave me a cold look. "We've talked about this already. You shouldn't be walking at night."

"I'm a big girl, alright?"

"And there are bigger men who would do terrible things to you."

I didn't need his protection or his advice, so I dropped it. "I just prefer the hotel. I don't want to see your place or become acquainted with it."

He looked out the driver's side window and stared at the cinder block he parked in front of. "You say you aren't interested in a relationship, but it looks like you're doing everything you possibly can to avoid one. You're too scared to get close to anyone, so you put up roadblocks at every turn."

"That's not true—"

"Then let's go upstairs." He got out of the car and left me behind.

I stayed in the passenger seat of his car and closed my eyes, wishing I'd never agreed to dinner in the first place. Now I was in a situation I didn't want to be in. I finally pushed the door open and stepped out.

He was leaning against the trunk. "If you really want me to take you back, I will. But I won't be joining you."

"So, if I want to get laid, I have to stay here?"

"Yes." He walked ahead of me and headed to the elevator doors before he stepped inside.

If I had any restraint, I would just go home and forget about this night. I would use my hand instead or find another guy to fill my nights.

But there was only one Hades Lombardi.

The elevator rose and carried us to the lower level of his home. He stepped out first into the empty house and headed for the circular stairway to the right. No servants popped out, and he didn't offer to give me a tour.

Full of shame, I followed him.

His bedroom was on the top floor, with a private patio that had a perfect view of the cathedral. My house was visible from this angle, a building just a few miles west. His bedroom chambers were grand like his home was from the Victorian age, even though this place had to have been renovated in the least ten years.

Once the bedroom door was shut and we had our privacy, he pulled his shirt over his head and left it on the floor, probably because it was someone else's responsibility to pick it up when he went to work tomorrow. He unbuttoned his jeans and got undressed, stripping down until he was naked—and hard.

When I looked at his sculpted physique, his explosive arms and his brick house of a chest, I forgot about that long dinner, forgot about the exchange between Hades and Damien. I even forgot about how he didn't go to the hotel like I asked. In front of me was nothing but man, God's perfect creation. Men weren't bred this way. They weren't constructed to be so hard and tough, but so damn beautiful at the same time.

Nothing outside the two of us mattered. We were just a man and a woman, two bodies that belonged together. My fingers automatically unzipped the back of my dress as I watched him, mesmerized by the hot look in his eyes. I let the fabric fall to the floor and dropped the bra with it. Then my thong was pushed over my ass so it could join the pile.

His eyes combed me over, his dick hardening just a little more at the sight of me.

I slowly walked toward him, feeling my heart race like I feared for my life. My bare feet hit the soft rug on the floor, and I slowly sauntered to him, feeling like the sexiest thing in the world when he looked at me like that.

I walked up to him, and without taking another breath, my fingers dug into his hair and I kissed him. My body balanced on my tiptoes so I could bring our bodies closer together, and I kissed him like I loved him, not despised him.

His hand cupped my cheek then snaked into my hair, fisting it so he could control me, so he could deepen the kiss or pin me down. His other arm wrapped around my waist, the metal of his watch digging into my skin.

The kiss was so good, I didn't mind it.

I breathed into his mouth as my fingers explored him, as I felt the muscles of his body, felt his strength at my fingertips. His skin was so warm, burning from the heat of his muscles.

My fingers returned to his hair, and I pulled him closer, getting so lost in him that I forgot what day it was...what year it was. The connection I felt with this man made me forget reality, made me forget who I was.

Because all I could think about was us.

He guided me to the bed, his hand grabbing my ass as he lifted me then laid me down.

His bed was so comfortable, much better than the hard mattress at the hotel. The sheets were soft like satin, and my body immediately dipped under his weight. I sank deep underneath him, conquered by this man who professed to be a king.

He rolled a condom on then fucked me.

My knees were pushed to my chest, and his face hung above mine as he ground his hips into me. His hands were balled into fists as he held himself on top of me. His muscled ass clenched tightly as he shoved himself inside me, pressing me farther into the mattress with every thrust.

I breathed against his mouth and moaned, my toes already curling in ecstasy. This was exactly what I wanted when I woke up that morning. This was exactly the sex I craved. I wanted him to do all the work, to give it to me good and slow so I could enjoy it while our mouths moved together.

His lips slid to my neck and he kissed me softly, still fucking me with perfect precision. His mouth slowly moved up to my ear, and he whispered through his heavy breathing, "You're fucking beautiful."

My fingers dug into his hair, sliding through the sweat that dripped down his neck to his back. "God…"

He rested his forehead against mine and kept rocking, this

time gluing his eyes to mine. With every thrust, he gave me all of him, gave me every single inch so I could feel just how hard he was. "This pussy... Jesus."

I held on to him tighter, feeling my legs open as he hit the perfect spot. Every time we hooked up, I went home later and later. We seemed to crave each other more, not less. Our passion turned into something combustible. We couldn't stop. Not for anything, not for anyone. We were both addicted. "Don't stop...don't ever stop."

7

HADES

Shirtless and barefoot, I sat on the patio with my cup of black coffee on the table in front of me. It was ten in the morning, four hours later than I usually woke up. My hand dragged down my face as I tried to wake up, to get my brain to function normally.

I didn't take Sofia home until three.

I tried to get her to stay—but she refused.

I had so much shit to do today, but I blew it all off.

This woman was destroying me.

My phone rang, and Damien's name appeared on the screen.

I declined his call. I already knew how that conversation was going to go.

Don't ignore me, asshole. His text message popped up instantly.

I turned the phone over altogether.

A few minutes later, my bedroom door opened, and Damien walked inside, looking stealthy in his black Armani suit. He looked through the open doors to my patio, his eyebrows furrowed like he wanted to pull a gun out and shoot me. "You've got to be kidding me."

I finally picked up my mug and took a drink.

Damien reached the table and turned my phone over. "Fuck you too."

"How did you get in here?"

"Shut up, Helena loves me."

"I don't love you."

"Asshole, you love me more." He sat in the chair across from me and stared at me like I was a talking frog. "What the hell happened today?"

"I told Ana to cancel my meetings."

"Because...?" He looked around. "You decided to take a sick day? Bitch, you ain't sick."

I rubbed the migraine from my temple. "Could you just shut up for two seconds?"

"No. I don't shut up when my business partner blows me off."

"I didn't blow you off. I just had a long night last night."

"Why? Did the Skull Kings pull something?"

"No."

"Okay...did someone put a hit on you?"

"No."

"Did the cops—"

"No. Nothing happened, alright? I just didn't sleep well last night."

"Poor baby didn't get any sleep?" he asked sarcastically. "Come on, you're fucking Hades. Don't pull that pussy shit on me. Speaking of pussy, if you fucked that fine piece of ass last night, you should have slept hard."

Sofia was just a woman I was screwing, but I felt protective of her, even a little possessive. "Don't talk about her like that."

He leaned back and nodded his head slowly. "I get it now... She kept you up all night."

I'd never had such an intense relationship with a woman before, someone I couldn't keep my hands off for more than a few minutes. I wanted to keep fucking her forever. It wasn't just about the sex, the pleasure for my dick, the cosmic orgasms... It was so much more. The heat between us burned me from the inside out. Every kiss, every touch... It was fucking cocaine. I'd never had an addiction my whole life...until now.

Damien kept watching me. "You blew off work for a woman?"

"I didn't blow off anything. I just didn't wake up."

"Because of her."

"No. I took her home at three. It was my choice to sleep in. Don't blame her. And stop grilling me, asshole. I run this empire with the same efficiency, whether I'm awake, asleep, or dead. Chill the fuck out."

"You didn't tell me about her. What's that about?"

"Despite what you think, I don't tell you everything."

"Uh, yes, you do."

I looked away and ignored him.

"You tell me about every hot piece of ass that falls into your lap. You tell me about every heart you break, every cherry you pop—"

"She didn't tell me she was a virgin. She lied, alright? I never would have done that shit if I'd known. It's trashy."

"Whatever. You tell me everything. But this one...silence. What does that mean?"

I still wouldn't look at him. I chose to examine the activity of the city, the bells tolling in the distance, the cars driving down narrow streets. Sofia was probably at the hotel right now, showing up to work on time even though Gustavo wasn't even there. That was the kind of integrity she had. "It means nothing."

"I think it means something. It wouldn't worry so much if you would just admit it."

I didn't know how I felt about this woman. I'd never been so coldly rejected by a woman before. She'd walked away from me so many times, was so repulsed by the idea of spending time with me that I couldn't wrap my head around it. Women would do anything to be with me, but Sofia didn't give a damn. I could see her perception of me every time I looked at her. I was just some cocky playboy that didn't give a damn about anyone.

Was she right?

Why did I care?

The more she pushed me away, the more I wanted her.

And every time the clothes came off...damn. She definitely wanted me then, definitely gave me the kind of connection I could easily get addicted to. She fulfilled my fantasies. She obliterated the memory of every other woman. She was the sexiest woman in my bed, the most gorgeous woman between my sheets.

I didn't want anyone else but her.

That'd never happened before.

Damien kept watching me. "You listening, asshole?"

"I'm always listening. Doesn't mean I pay attention."

He looked away for a while, thinking to himself. When he became serious, he sighed and looked at me again. "How long have you been seeing her?"

"About three weeks..." We just went to the hotel and hooked up. Most of the time, conversations didn't even take place. Last night was the most I'd gotten from her, but it was like pulling teeth.

"Three weeks... That's a long time."

Really? It felt like the blink of an eye.

"Is it more than a fling?"

I didn't want to stop seeing her. In fact, I wanted to see her more. I wanted to see as much of her as possible. Since the first moment I saw her at that party, I was mesmerized. I was obsessed. She was fucking beautiful. "No."

"Then I don't understand—"

"I want it to be more than that. She doesn't."

Damien turned quiet, letting those words sink in. "And what do you want it to be?"

"I don't know...but she won't give me a chance."

"Wow. A woman turned you down?"

"She only wants sex from me. Every time I push for more, she shoots me down."

"And I bet that drives you crazy."

I didn't like it. "A bit."

"Is she married or something?"

"No."

"Hmm..."

"And she doesn't want to get married. She doesn't want a relationship at all."

"I've never heard of that," Damien said. "Women are always looking for something serious. At least, that's my experience."

"Mine too."

"So Hades has fallen for the one woman who doesn't want him."

That night in Morocco flooded back to me. I didn't give it much merit at the time, even though she knew my name. And I didn't think she was right about any of it, until I became the biggest drug dealer in the south of Europe and took a turn for the dark side. I thought it was just coincidence. Hopefully, it still was. "I'm not in love with her."

"It looks like you're going in that direction."

"You're jumping to conclusions."

He shrugged. "I've known you for a long time, Hades. Not once has anything like this ever happened. You talk about women like they are single-use plastic bags. They're used and then tossed. But you're working your ass off to get this woman to give you a few minutes of her time. You're blowing off work... That's not you."

She brought out the worst in me.

"Maybe you should forget about her before it gets any worse."

That was the logical thing to do, but I couldn't picture my life without her in it. I didn't want to go back to the bar and pick up a random woman. I wanted to see Sofia's face looking up at me while I drove her into the sheets. I wanted her pussy—only her pussy. "I don't want to forget about her."

He chuckled. "Then I don't know what you should do. It sounds like you can never have her."

I knew exactly what kind of man I was. I never gave up on anything. When I didn't get what I wanted, I just found another way. And if there were no other way, I would make one. Sofia was no different. Maybe I couldn't take her like I owned her.

Maybe I had to earn her first.

I DIDN'T TEXT her before I arrived at the hotel.

I could never turn down an invitation from her, and I knew she couldn't turn me down either.

I walked into the lobby and saw her standing at the counter, her black hair pulled into a tight ponytail. Her high cheekbones were brushed with blush, her lips were red like a good wine, and her eyelashes were thick like a doll's. She stood there like a queen, her shoulders back and her slender neck straight. If there were a tiara on her head, it would never fall.

She was perfect.

I approached her desk and ignored the stares from the women at the counter.

When Sofia heard my footsteps, she looked up. Her polite smile was replaced by a hard stare, almost cold. But her eyes burned with fire, burned like the sight of me made her heart flutter.

I approached the counter. "Do you have any space for two people in the restaurant?"

She was still at first, as if she didn't know how to react to my request. Then she went through the motions and gave me a bullshit response. "Yes, I can get you a reservation for tonight. How does nine sound?"

"Perfect." I walked to the elevators and went to my room.

Room 402.

I stripped down to my boxers and sat in the armchair near the window. The floor-to-ceiling windows provided a phenomenal view of the city, of the bright lights of the Catholic churches and the restaurants along the main street. I could see my building not too far from here.

I held the glass of scotch in my hand and took a sip as I examined the world at my feet. At this very moment, my crystal was being sold in the alleyways between buildings, in Greek Isles while vacationers enjoyed the crystal-blue water. To anyone else, the streets seemed quiet, the people seemed innately good. But in reality...I controlled every corner of this place.

I had enemies like everyone else. The Skull Kings wanted a cut of my profits in exchange for territory, but I refused to give in. They were the middlemen in the transaction, and that shit didn't fly. But they didn't move against me because that was a war neither one of us would win. They stayed out of my business—and I stayed out of theirs.

Sofia was too innocent for this shit. She was a grown woman who could handle herself, but she had unrealistic expectations of the world. She assumed her hotel operated as an honest business, but it was flooded with blood money. With the kind of integrity she had, she should be doing something else with her time. Maybe I should tell her...or maybe Gustavo would chase her off somehow.

I'd just started to fantasize about fucking her from behind, her ass in my hands, when the door opened.

She stepped inside, her stilettos tapping lightly against the floor as she entered the room. She stripped off her jacket and hung it over the back of the chair, her seductive gaze on me. Her stare started at my muscular thighs and slowly moved up my frame, gradually taking in my chiseled appearance.

The only thing on her mind was sex.

Nothing more, nothing less.

It was the exact same way I'd looked at so many women in the past. I wanted silent conversations and loud moans. I wanted to have the most passionate sex possible then walk away like it never happened in the first place. The last thing I wanted to do was listen to a woman's daddy problems, listen to them confess their deepest feelings.

I didn't give a damn.

That was exactly how this woman felt about me. I was just a hard dick that got her off.

I set my glass down and rose to my feet, keeping my mouth shut like she wanted. I moved closer to her and located the zipper along her ass. I unzipped it while keeping my eyes on her, listening to her skirt fall to the floor. My fingers attacked her shirt next, stripping it off and taking her bra with it.

I pulled her into my chest then grabbed the band in her hair. I yanked it free, causing her smooth hair to cascade around her shoulders. The hair tie snapped in half and fell to the floor along with her clothes.

She stayed still, letting me have her however I wanted.

I stared down into her hair, my fingers playing with the

strands as I kept her close to me. Our foreheads came together as we stood in front of the window, naked and close together like we were a single person.

Her arms hooked around my neck, and her lips hovered near mine, plump and red from her favorite shade of lipstick. Without feeling my mouth or my cock, she moaned...like she'd been looking forward to this since the moment she saw me in the lobby...maybe even before that.

A woman's desire was the sexiest thing in the world, but for the last ten years, I'd been taking it for granted. All women wanted me, so it didn't matter. Watching Sofia tremble for me, visibly go weak because she was in my arms, was a different kind of reward. It made me feel like a man...to please the woman I actually gave a damn about. Sex was the only thing anchoring her to me, keeping her coming back for more. Once I lost that, I lost her.

I didn't want to lose her.

We'd been fucking for a while, so I knew exactly what she liked. I knew what really drove her wild, what made her so weak she could barely say a few words. I wanted to fuck her like a dog and stare at that sexy asshole, but she loved having me on top, loved digging her nails into my back while I did all the work. It made her bottom lip tremble like she was about to cry, made her whimper hysterically.

A real man knew what his woman liked without asking. And he always gave it to her as much as she wanted, because pleasing her was better than any dirty fantasy he had. I backed her up to the bed then fell onto the sheets with her. The comforter was already pulled down, and the extra pillows were put to the side. It was ready for fucking. I lay on top of her, her hair stretching across the pillow. Her lips were parted with her deep breaths, and her eyes were so bright with their beautiful fire. I hadn't kissed her once, and she was practically begging for it. The last time we were together was a shitshow, but she seemed to have forgotten it.

My body got into the perfect position for fucking, keeping her legs wide apart so my dick had perfect access to her wet cunt. My shaft pressed against her pussy and felt the slickness already oozing.

She'd come within at least a minute. She was so hard up, I wasn't sure what she needed me for. Her clit was a button, and all I had to do was press it to make her explode.

When I didn't pull on a condom and slide inside her, she groaned in frustration. "Fuck me already." She bit her bottom lip because the command turned her on a little more. She didn't hide her enthusiasm even if it humiliated her.

"I'm fucking you without a condom."

"What?" she blurted, still under the haze of desire.

"No condom."

"Are you crazy?"

"I'm clean. Just got tested. You?"

Her nails scratched my back as she squeezed my hips with her thighs. She was such a pragmatic person who could make the best decisions, but since her nipples were hard as diamonds because she was so horny, she couldn't think straight. "Just put on a condom and fuck me."

"No."

"Jesus Christ, Hades. When has a woman ever asked you to fuck her and you ignored her?"

"Are you seeing anyone else?" This was the only way I would get what I wanted out of her. If we skipped protection, that meant there would be no one else, just us two. It wouldn't be a relationship, but it would be something. At least she would be mine.

"What kind of question is that? I don't ask you that."

"I'm not seeing anyone. And if you aren't either, let's do this right. I want to come inside you." I pressed my forehead to hers and ground my shaft against her sensitive clit. "I want to keep going...fill your pussy with so much come that we stain these sheets. I want your panties to smell like me for days. I want you to feel me explode inside you, feel how much I want you."

Her eyes glazed over when she imagined everything I described.

"Now, answer me." I kissed her softly on the mouth, our lips moving together in a gentle dance. I slowly ground against her, giving her a taste of how I would feel if we were just skin-to-skin, if we were nothing but man and woman.

"No..." She spoke between kisses. "I'm not seeing anyone."

My cock twitched as it continued to pulse against her. I got the answer I wanted, got a commitment from her that she didn't want to give me. I had to use sex as a weapon, but it worked. I pressed my fingers against the top of my shaft then guided the head of my dick inside her.

Jesus fucking Christ.

My crown was introduced to her salty slickness, and the millions of nerves at the tip fired off in pleasure. The head squeezed as I moved in, feeling the tightness and the moisture suffocate it immediately.

Her nails started to dig as she moaned.

I could slide inside so easily because I'd been fucking her for almost a month, but I took my sweet-ass time because it felt so damn good. This pussy was so sweet, tight, and fuckable. My dick moved right in, claiming the territory as his in perpetuity. My ass tightened as I sank a little deeper, as my balls came into contact with the wetness that was now slathered all over my shaft.

Fuck.

Her fingers dug into my hair, and she breathed against my mouth, so far gone in this bliss that she could barely breathe. Her legs wrapped around my waist and anchored me against her, forming a rope that bound me to her forever. Her thighs shook slightly against me, her body overtaken by shivers.

I could feel it too...that connection that brought us together over and over. It was red-hot heat and addictive desire. I was so damn hot for her, and she was scorching for me. Combined together, we were every addictive drug on the market mixed together. Potent and dangerous, it had the ability to kill us both if we weren't careful.

But she squeezed me to her like she didn't want me to be careful.

I started to thrust, using regular strokes to drive deep inside her. I was pushing myself into the most addictive pussy I'd ever had, so tight and so wet. I intended to be there all night, giving her load after load, not catching a moment of sleep because I'd rather be here...fucking this pussy.

It only took her a couple seconds to climax, to squeeze my hips with her thighs and shiver from her head to her toes. Her nails sliced my back, and she whimpered against my lips, a few tears springing from her eyes because it felt so good.

Fuck. My hips bucked harder all on their own, and I drove myself into a climax I couldn't prevent. My biological imperative as a man took over, so now I needed to come after watching her get off. I needed to fill that pussy with seed.

I kept myself deep inside her and released, giving an involuntary grunt of pleasure. I'd come inside her before, but the tip of the condom always caught my deposit. Now I was adding my stickiness to her own, mixing our come together. I pushed her deeper into the mattress as I finished, knowing I gave her more than she could possibly handle.

When I finished, she brought my mouth to hers and kissed me harder, as if my come turned her on all over again. Her hand went to my ass, and she pressed me deeper into her, making me fuck her even at half-mast. "I want more...give me more."

"It's four in the morning. I have to go..." She sat up and tried to move out of bed.

I'd just gotten hard again, so she wasn't going anywhere. "No." I grabbed her by the arm and dragged her back to me.

My hand slid into her hair, and I kissed her, using my best moves to get her to stay. Within a minute, she softened for me, giving up the fight because she couldn't possibly win.

I pulled her onto my lap and guided her up and down.

She moaned when she felt my large dick move in and out, sliding through all the loads I'd already given her throughout the night. Her palms pressed against my chest for balance, and she rolled her hips over and over, taking that dick like a whore who needed cash.

I touched her tits as she fucked me, enjoyed the sight of this beautiful woman dancing on my lap. She bounced up and down then rolled her hips, giving me a show I could jerk off to a million times.

I rubbed her clit with my thumb and brought her to orgasm before I followed.

Now, I was done.

She rolled over and lay beside me, her eyes immediately closing because we'd only slept a couple hours since we'd met at nine the evening before. Her hair wasn't as shiny as it had been earlier because it was soaked with sweat like she'd gone to the gym.

Her pussy was full, though.

After a minute of relaxing, she sat up and looked at the time. "Shit…"

If she would just come to my place, this would be easier. She wouldn't have to sneak out of the hotel without being seen. She could sleep in and take a couple days off so she would be in bed by the time I finished work for the day.

"My mother's gonna get a kick out of this." She picked up her clothes off the floor and started to get dressed.

"How does your mother know if you haven't been home all night?"

"Because that woman knows everything."

I sat up and leaned against the headboard. "And did you tell her about me?"

"No." She pulled on her bra and panties then zipped up her skirt.

"She thinks you're out with different guys?"

"I don't know what she thinks. She doesn't ask questions."

That was interesting.

She put on her blouse and smoothed out the wrinkles against her chest. "She's encouraging me to get this out of my system now. That's her one regret in life...marrying too young and not fucking around enough."

A slow grin stretched across my face. "She seems wise."

She rolled her eyes in a playful way. "She says it'll be easier for me to marry someone appropriate if I get all this out of my system, so she doesn't care." She walked to the mirror on the wall and started fixing her appearance, starting with her crazy hair.

"That must be nice."

"Yeah, but it's still weird to talk about. I need to get my own place."

"I can buy you something."

She turned to me and gave me the coldest look. "I should be the one giving you money—paying for your manwhore services."

Most men would take that as a compliment, but since I had a different agenda with her, it wasn't exactly what I wanted to hear. It implied she was using me for sex...because she didn't want anything else from me.

"I don't need your money. I can afford my own apartment now, so I'll find something soon."

I intended to steer her away from these hookups at the hotel. I wanted her in my bed or somewhere else more private. This still felt like a dirty affair that we were hiding from our spouses, but if we were just sleeping with each other, it was time to upgrade.

I got out of bed and prepared to walk her to the door.

She grabbed her purse and turned to me. "I guess I'll see you later."

"Yes, you will." My arms slid around her, and I pulled her against my chest so I could kiss her goodbye.

She melted at my touch, like the previous insults had never come from her mouth.

I drew back and let her go, reluctantly.

She looked up at me, as if she had something else to say.

I stared at her as I waited.

"I don't know what happened earlier... I think we were just—"

"It's you and me—no one else." I silenced her insecurities.

"However long this lasts, I want it to be just us. If we're gonna do this, we may as well enjoy every single moment until it's gone. I want all of you—not just a piece of you."

This would be the moment where she would argue with me, tell me I didn't have any part of her. But this time, she let it go, probably because that night of sex was so good that she wasn't going to stop. She wanted it skin-to-skin, wanted to feel my come fill her up like an empty tank needing gas at the pump. "Alright...until it's gone." She was in her heels, so she didn't have to rise onto her tiptoes to kiss me goodbye. It was the first time she'd done that, gave me any kind of affection that wasn't purely sexual.

It was a start.

I squeezed her ass before I let her go.

She turned around and walked out, shaking that ass like she was torturing me on purpose. She left without looking at me again, letting the door shut behind her. Once her presence was gone from the room, it immediately felt lonely, like a cold draft had just erased her warmth.

I sat in the armchair once more and sipped the scotch I'd been enjoying the night before. The sun would rise in a few hours and I was exhausted, but after the night I'd had, I didn't want it to end.

There had been only one time in my life when I didn't wear a condom...and it was with her.

How could I ever go back?

My phone started to ring from my pants on the floor. I fished it out, saw Damien's name on the screen, and answered it. It was four in the morning, so he would only call me at this hour if it was important. "What?"

"You sound wide awake."

"I'm always awake."

"Really?" he countered. "Because you didn't show up to work a couple days ago because—"

"What do you want, Damien?"

He dropped the argument and turned serious. "Maddox wants a meeting."

"Why?"

"He wants to renegotiate territory."

Maddox was my biggest competitor. His product was similar to mine but not quite as pure. If he had the chance to take me out, he would. I'd do the same to him. We were enemies, bloodthirsty for each other's corpse. He was a decade older than me, and when I came into the game, he didn't take me seriously. Considered me to be a child. But I rose in power overnight and pulled territory from directly under his feet. It started a war, battles lost on both sides, and there was no end in sight. "Not gonna happen."

"Just passing along the message. Do I deny his request?"

"I have nothing to say to him. This is my territory. He can take his business elsewhere."

Damien accepted my decision. "Alright...but there will be consequences."

"I'd judge him if there weren't."

8

SOFIA

I STOOD AT THE COUNTER IN THE LOBBY OF THE HOTEL, waiting for time to pass so my shift would end. I was grateful I had a job because it paid my bills and got me an apartment a few blocks away. After I moved in, I'd finally get some independence back.

Wouldn't have to do the walk of shame right in front of my mother.

It was just another receptionist and me since it was late at night. After seven in the evening, people didn't enter the lobby unless it was the weekend and they'd spent the night out on the town. So when I saw a group of men walk in, all wearing suits, it was odd.

There was one clearly in the lead, wearing a dark blue suit. With a rigid back and a cold demeanor, he entered the hotel with a clear purpose, marching across the lobby under the chandeliers, and heading toward the lounge. I didn't know every single guest staying at the hotel, but I usually could surmise their purpose. Businessmen were there during the day, sometimes meeting a client for lunch. Businessmen in the evening were usually having an affair with a woman half their age while their pregnant wife waited for them to come home.

These men didn't fit into either category.

They entered the lounge then disappeared.

Since this was my hotel, I was naturally nosy, so I took a break from my desk to see what they were up to. The lounge was down the hall and in the corner, where there were huge windows that showed the entire street. I stepped inside and noticed similarly dressed men already sitting at a table in the center of the lounge—and no one was around.

The air felt heavy, like I'd stepped into a meeting I wasn't part of.

I lingered there for a moment but couldn't make out the conversation. They were speaking too quietly.

The bartender wasn't even there.

What was going on?

One man in the corner noticed me. He stared at me for a while, his eyes narrowed as if he was the school bully and I was his next target. "Can we help you?"

All heads turned my way. Smoke from their cigars drifted to the ceiling, and their glasses of booze rested next to their hands. They must have helped themselves to the bar as if they could do whatever they wanted. My first impulse was to say something sassy, like usual, but my gut told me that wasn't a good idea.

That my life depended on it.

"I noticed there wasn't a bartender. Do you guys need anything?"

The guy who interrogated me dropped his guard slightly. "We're good, honey. Run along now."

Honey?

Run along now?

It took all my strength to turn around and walk away. But I knew I was making the right call.

———

THE SECOND I walked in the door, I slipped off my heels so I wouldn't have to wear them a moment longer. Heels and stairs didn't go together, so that was a problem I wanted to avoid. If my feet had lips, they'd be screaming in relief right now.

My mother appeared out of the shadows...because she was a damn gargoyle. "Home at a reasonable hour... That's a nice change."

"Hello, Mother," I said sarcastically. "So nice to see you lingering in the entranceway."

"You can't wait to move out tomorrow, huh?" She was perfectly aware of my annoyance, but she managed to brush it off like a joke.

"A bit."

"Gustavo and I will miss you."

"No, you won't," I jabbed.

She chuckled. "Yeah, probably not. But it is nice that you'll be close by. So, how was work?"

"You know...boring." I considered telling her about the strange men who crashed the lounge, but Gustavo was probably the better recipient of news like that.

"You aren't seeing your mystery man tonight?"

"What makes you think I have a mystery man?"

"Well, I hope you aren't out until three in the morning with all different men..."

I headed to the stairs and began the climb.

"So...who is he?"

"You're being nosy, Ma."

"I'm just curious. Is this serious? If it is, you know—"

"It's not serious, so let's not even go there."

"Oh, I see." She wore a long nightgown and lifted it above her feet as she walked. "Then he must be a fun mistake."

He wasn't fun, and he wasn't a mistake. He was just...a good memory. At least, someday he would be. It was a passionate relationship that I would never find again, and I wanted to hold on to it until the flames went out. My heart was locked up tight, so no one could come anywhere near it. Hades would never hurt me because it wasn't possible. How could a man break your heart if he never had your heart in the first place? "Something like that."

"I miss being young. Have so many good memories..."

"Yes, you say that a lot." We made it to the second landing, and I turned to say goodnight. "I'll see you in the morning. I've got to soak my feet in the tub."

"Alright, honey. Good night."

THE MOVERS PLACED ALL the furniture in my new apartment, and I spent the afternoon unpacking everything from the boxes. It was a small one-bedroom apartment, so I had a little kitchen, a four-person dining table, and a couch. It wasn't as grand as my mother's mansion, but it still beat living with her.

Esme lifted the dishes out of the box and set them on the counter. "So, should we celebrate with a bottle of wine here or go out?"

"I do have wine here, but there are no hot guys here."

She chuckled. "That's a very good point."

Now that Hades was the regular man in my bed, I wasn't looking for anyone new. But I knew Esme was hitting guys out of the park. She lived the epic single lifestyle. She didn't want to be cooped up in my apartment when she had sexy legs to show off. "You wanna go out, then?"

"Only if you pick up a hot guy too."

"You know, I'm not really looking right now. I'm just focusing on me." I pulled the blankets out of the box and draped them over the couches. When I didn't hear the rattle of the dishes anymore, I looked at Esme again.

She gave me a look that clearly said, "You're full of shit."

"What?"

"Aren't looking?" she asked. "People only say that if they're already seeing someone. Are you seeing someone?"

No, I wasn't seeing Hades. We just weren't seeing other people because we were skipping protection. It wasn't a romantic decision. "No."

"Then you're picking up a hot guy."

"I'm not doing that either."

"So, you are seeing someone."

"No..."

She cocked an eyebrow. "Spill it."

I tossed the blankets aside and joined her in the kitchen. "It's not how it seems, alright?" I grabbed a couple of plates and placed them in the cabinets over the stove. "I'm hooking up with this guy, but we're exclusive for the moment."

"Uh-huh..." She propped one hand on her hip, giving me so much attitude, it was suffocating. "That sounds like a relationship."

"It's not," I said firmly. "We just don't want to use protection. That's all."

"And why wouldn't you want to use protection if this guy means nothing to you?"

"Come on," I said as I rolled my eyes. "Don't make me get into the details. I'm not interested in him romantically. Not at all. He's not my type."

"Not your type? You're sleeping with him, aren't you?"

"I have needs, obviously. But that's it. My point is, I can't pick up any hot guy I see."

"Then he must be pretty good in bed if you're willing to swear off all other men temporarily."

She wouldn't believe me if I told her. "Yeah…he's pretty good."

"Am I gonna meet this guy?"

"No. He's not gonna meet anyone."

"So, he feels the same way? About this being casual?"

"Yes." He didn't strike me as the boyfriend type. I really knew nothing about him, but I wanted it to stay that way.

She finished putting away the dishes. "Alright, let's get a drink. Hearing all this talk about good, casual, exclusive sex makes me want it too."

———

IT WAS mid-November so it was too cold outside not to wear a coat. We shed our jackets at the front then found a vacant booth. We ordered our drinks and got to talking.

"How's the hotel?" she asked. "Gustavo still got a tampon up his ass?"

"Yeah, a bit. Technically, the hotels aren't even his—they belong to my mother."

"Asshole."

I was annoyed by the situation, but I did think Gustavo was a good guy. "My mother agrees...that's what the problem is. Until I have a strong husband, I'll never have any real responsibilities there."

"She needs to build a time machine and go back to 1734."

I laughed when I imagined my mother getting into some contraption that actually transported her to a different time period. Her morals were so archaic that I didn't understand where she got them. Was it really by choice?

"So, on a scale of one to ten, how good is this guy in bed?"

"Wow..."

"What?" she asked. "I'm your best friend. I can ask."

I stirred my vodka cranberry and stared down at my swirling ice just to have something to do.

"Girl," she pressed. "Just give me a number, one to ten."

I took a long drink before I put down the glass. "Eleven."

"Ooh." She leaned forward and clapped her hands against the table. "Does he have a brother? Tell me he has a brother. A cousin will do."

"You know...I don't know."

"You don't know what?"

"If he has a brother. I've never asked."

Esme furrowed her eyebrows. "Wow...you really don't talk, huh? All you do is screw."

"That's how I like it."

"How do you know he really is faithful?" she asked. "Since you hardly know him."

I shrugged. "I guess I don't know. I just think we're screwing so much that I doubt he's looking for sex elsewhere. And this is a short-term fling. It's not that hard to be committed to someone for a month or whatever."

"What are you going to do when it's over?" she asked. "Where are you going to find another eleven?"

My lungs deflated from all the air I had been holding. "I don't think I ever will."

"God, that's depressing."

"Yeah…" When I slept with someone else, I knew I would be disappointed. "So, do you see anyone you like?" I took the attention off of me and my amazing sex life. Maybe Esme was inspired to find her eleven out there. I hadn't even glanced at the other people in the bar because it didn't matter who was there. I wasn't going home with anyone, so I didn't even want a free drink.

"Ooh…he's gorgeous."

"Which one?"

"He's in the back, sitting with a bunch of guys. Some are older, which is weird. But he's the one with the chocolate-colored eyes and that sexy shadow on his face." She nodded to the other side of the bar, which was about a hundred feet away.

My eyes zeroed in on a face I instantly recognized. Hades

was there, having drinks with an eclectic group of men. Some were middle-aged; some were even old. He seemed to be the youngest guy there, looking sexy in a leather jacket with a gray V-neck underneath. At least he wasn't here alone or with Damien, picking up women. He seemed to be doing business of some kind.

"That's the sexiest guy I've ever seen. He's drinking scotch... I like a man who knows how to drink. I think I'll bring him a double to break the ice."

It was so awkward that I didn't want to tell her the truth. "Actually...that's him."

Esme looked back at me, her eyes filled with confusion. "Who?"

"Eleven..."

"Oh my god, shut your ass."

"Nope, I can't."

"That's the guy you're sleeping with?" She raised her palm in the air. "Girl, good for you."

I chuckled before I gave her a high five. Of course, Esme wasn't embarrassed by the situation. She had the confidence to bounce back no matter what. "Yeah, he's easy on the eyes."

"I can tell he earned that score. Look at those shoulders."

"They look better when he's naked."

She chuckled. "You're so dirty. What's he doing with all those dudes?"

"Probably working."

"What does he do?"

"Runs a bank or something."

"So, he's rich?" she asked in surprise.

"Yeah. Pretty loaded." Based on his house, his car, and the fact that he owned a restaurant…he was doing pretty well.

"Well, now is the perfect chance for you to see if he would keep his word."

"What do you mean?"

"I doubt he's seen us from way over there. He looks preoccupied. What if I hit on him and see what happens?"

Testing him had never crossed my mind. "I don't know… It doesn't really matter what he does."

"Doesn't matter?" she asked incredulously. "You're screwing that guy bareback."

"Yeah, but most men cheat on their wives, so we're constantly exposed. He seems like a guy who would take care of himself if he wasn't committed."

She gave me the weirdest look. "You weren't kidding when you said he meant nothing to you."

"I didn't say that, exactly. It's just, we aren't in a relationship. If he does take you up on your offer, it doesn't mean anything. Maybe he'll say yes to you, and then he'll break it off with me because he's officially bored with me. It just doesn't mean anything like it would if he were my boyfriend. You get what I'm saying?"

"I suppose." She turned back to look at him. "But I'm still

interested in seeing what he does..." She set down her drink and was about to slide out of the booth when some other woman appeared. "Never mind. We'll find out anyway."

We couldn't overhear their conversation, but the girl only had eyes for Hades, which made sense because he was the only young guy in the group. They conversed for a while, and then she walked off.

"Well..." Esme turned back to me. "Look at that."

"He's working. She picked the wrong time."

"So, you think he would have gone for it if he weren't?"

My gut told me he wouldn't, that he wouldn't have even bothered pressuring me unless he were serious about it. But I also understood that I really didn't know Hades...at all. We had explosive chemistry and a connection that went all the way down into my bones, and for some reason, that seemed to be enough reason to trust him. "Probably not."

———

Two guys came over to talk to us, and I felt bad for the guy who picked me because I was already taken. But Esme seemed to hit it off with the man who came over and bought her a drink. They talked for a while, laughed, and even shared a few kisses.

"So, you wanna get out of here?" The guy next to me was handsome, had enough looks that he could probably get away with that behavior with someone else. But I wasn't interested. I liked a bit of conversation before hitting the sheets.

"I'm seeing someone."

He nodded slowly. "No surprise there. Pretty girls are always taken."

I nodded to Esme. "She's not."

"Because she's so hot that she knows she doesn't need to settle." He slid out of the booth. "Nice meeting you."

He walked away and left me alone with Esme and her new boy toy. They were close together, her hand on his thigh as they shared a few heated embraces. Things were getting hot.

I should probably leave so I didn't look like a weirdo watching two people make out. I opened my clutch and set some cash on the table, when another guy sat next to me. One guy had just struck out, so another came up to bat.

"I was just leaving..." My words died in my mouth when his calm countenance came into my view. His jawline was covered by a thick shadow of hair, a deep color that matched his eyes. His leather jacket hid his muscular arms from view, but there was no doubt he was fit as hell.

His arm moved to the top of the booth, his fingertips immediately digging into the back of my neck. He leaned in slowly, his cologne surrounding me just the way it did in bed. Every time I left that hotel room, my clothes reeked of it. My mother had mentioned it so many times.

My reaction was instinctual. My hand reached for his thigh, and I squeezed it through his jeans as I felt his lips land on mine and kiss me. His fingers dug deeper into my hair as he cradled the back of my head, giving me tongue in a public place.

My fingers gripped his thigh tighter before sliding underneath his shirt and grazing up before touching his rock-hard stomach and chest. Images flashed in my mind of us together, naked and sweaty and grinding on a bed.

He ended the kiss and pulled his fingers from my hair. "Let's go."

ONCE WE WERE in my apartment, we went straight to bed. Clothes were ripped off, and we eagerly rushed until he was inside of me. Once his dick had successfully shoved itself deep within me, we both slowed way down.

My fingers dug into his hair, and I ground into him, moaning so loud because he felt so good.

Best dick ever.

Sex always seemed to be missionary, which I didn't mind because it was my favorite position. What woman didn't want a sexy man on top of her, kissing her and fucking her while she just had to enjoy it?

"Hades..." I was so lost in him that I said his name, so swept away in the goodness between my legs, I could hardly breathe. "God...Hades." My ankles locked around his waist, and I pulled him deeper into me, wanting every single inch before he came. My toes curled and ached as I came, as my pussy exploded around his dick.

My climax always seemed to bring him to the edge. He watched my little performance, watched me unravel until I was nothing but a body and hormones. Then he finished by releasing inside me, giving me a big load of come that I would keep all night.

I closed my eyes and relaxed, so satisfied I could fall asleep right then and there.

He gave me a final kiss before he slowly pulled out of me and rolled to the other side of the bed.

Having his bare dick inside me was so much better than the chafing latex of a condom. I wasn't sure I could ever go back...even after he was gone. I kicked the covers out from under me before pulling them up to my shoulder. The nice thing about screwing in my apartment was I didn't have to make the journey home.

He was the one who had to do it.

After he cooled off, he rolled toward me and hooked my leg over his hip, pressing our chests close together with our faces near each other. He watched me with his gorgeous eyes, took in my fatigued expression.

"If I fall asleep...just let yourself out."

"I'm not leaving." His hand snaked up my back and slowly moved into my hair. He was such a hard man who knew how to fuck, but he could be so gentle too. His hand cupped my cheek, and his thumb brushed across my bottom lip.

"Well, you aren't staying."

"I'm staying until morning." He defied me and didn't back down, like he somehow could call the shots even though this wasn't his place. "I'm tired of meeting at hotels and then heading home in the middle of the night. Not doing that anymore." His fingers returned to my hair, and he moved them into my strands, massaging my scalp.

I wanted to fight it, but I wouldn't win anyway. I was also too tired to really care. I wanted to kick him out just to set boundaries...not because I actually wanted him to leave. "Were you working?"

He nodded slightly. "And what were you doing?"

"Helping Esme get laid."

"I'm sure she can manage that on her own. You'll only disappoint the others when they realize they can't have you."

"Can't have me?"

He nodded. "You're mine." His fingers trailed down my back, over my ass, and along my leg. His eyes stared at me the same way as he did when he spotted me in the bar...like nothing else mattered.

"I'm not anybody's."

"My dick says otherwise." His hand stopped on my lower back and tugged me a little closer, making my tits press against his chest. "And you know I'm yours." He rested his face next to mine, bringing us so close together that we seemed to be more than just lovers.

Everything felt right, so I didn't argue with him. I let it be... and enjoyed it. This was the first time I'd been with a man who made me feel so much...so much passion...so much everything. That told me it wasn't a solid foundation, because real relationships needed more than sex and attraction. They needed truth, honesty, friendship... We didn't have any of that. We hardly knew each other. It was just...a dream.

"How's your week been?" he asked.

"The same. My stepfather thinks I'm inadequate."

"He doesn't think that."

"He doesn't give me any responsibilities."

"Maybe. But I assure you it's not because of your lack of qualities."

"Did he tell you this?" I didn't know what they talked about in private, but I didn't see how Hades could mention with me without explaining our relationship.

"No. I just know."

"I was there the other night, and I swear the mafia met in the lounge. It was like nine in the evening."

His caresses stopped, and his eyes focused intently. He was noticeably still. "What are you talking about?"

"A bunch of men in suits came in late and took over the lounge. Kicked out the bartender like they owned the place. I went in there to tell them off, but something told me to back off."

"Yes...you did the right thing."

"I told Gustavo, and he said I was exaggerating...but I wasn't. It's like he doesn't know anything about his own hotel. One guy kills himself, and then this? I mean, that's just strange."

Instead of asking a million questions like a normal person, he stayed quiet, his brain working behind his stoic gaze.

Minutes passed, and it seemed like he wouldn't say anything else about it.

"Do you know anything about that?"

He didn't blink. "I'm at the hotel very seldom." He didn't answer the question at all.

"So, is that a no?"

His eyes shifted back and forth as he looked into my gaze. "I'll talk to him about it. Let you know what I find out."

9

HADES

THE MEN OPENED THE STEEL DOORS, AND I STEPPED INSIDE TO the main floor of the operations building, hidden in plain sight in Florence. From the outside, it looked like an abandoned museum that was in such decay that it needed to be torn down. Inside was where we cooked our crystal, prepared it for shipment, and then distributed it by carriers on the ground or vehicles that drove it up north.

In the center of the room was one of my cooks.

He was dead.

A deep mark was around his throat where the noose had been tied, and his face was blue because he'd died of suffocation. His body was rigid since he'd been hanging by the rope for several hours after he was gone.

At least he hadn't been tortured.

Damien stood next to the body, his arms over his chest. "Found him hanging from the main bell of the cathedral this morning."

I already knew who was responsible.

Damien lifted his gaze and looked at me. "He's one of our best cooks. Now production will be halted." He waited for me to stay something. When I didn't, he pressed forward. "This was Maddox. Sending a message."

"Message received. He wants to be murdered." I lifted my gaze and looked at Damien. "I have alternate cooks in mind. They've been vetted. So we don't fall behind, I'll step in and finish the last batch."

Damien nodded. "Alright. What do we do about Maddox?"

"Not sure yet. But I'll think of something...and it'll be good."

I WENT to the Tuscan Rose to see Gustavo.

We had a lot to talk about.

I did my best to avoid Sofia. That woman was stealing all my nights, so she also was stealing all my days. I was always tired, always running on empty. But I wouldn't change a goddamn thing.

If I saw her in a tight skirt with a low-cut blouse, my professionalism would go to shit.

Thankfully, I got into his office without seeing her.

"Hades, to what do I owe the pleasure?" Gustavo stopped working on his computer and gave me all his attention. "Sorry about canceling a couple of weeks ago. That cold I had—"

"We have a problem with Sofia."

"Sofia?" He may not be related to her, but it was obvious he had affection for her just by how he said her name. He adored her. There was a picture of her on his desk, along with her mother.

"Yeah. She saw the mafia in the lounge."

He sighed. "Yeah, she told me about that. I told her that her eyes were playing tricks on her."

"If she's gonna work here, she needs to know what she's dealing with." I didn't want Sofia walking around oblivious to the true operations of this hotel. She had a big mouth, and that might land her in hot water.

He sighed loudly. "Sofia is never going to have a serious position here—"

"She's determined to change that. You aren't going to be able to shake her unless she knows the truth. Even if she never does have a part in the business, she's going to have to know the truth someday. She can't be naïve forever."

"It's not my place to tell her."

"Then you need to talk to her mother about it. Because Sofia is going to do something that's will put her in danger. She's got a moral compass and a strong sense of integrity. She's not going to like the truth. But she needs to hear it—and deal with it."

Gustavo listened to me and shook his head slightly. Then he lifted his gaze and looked at me again, this time with suspicion in his eyes. "How do you know all of this about Sofia?"

"Because she told me. We had a long conversation when you were ill. She's a very ambitious woman who wants to run this hotel someday. She needs to understand what she's working for. Maybe she'll want to walk away and pursue something else. That's her right."

"I understand, Hades."

"Or you need to fire her."

He chuckled. "Like that would work. How can you fire someone who doesn't have a real position?"

Nothing about this was funny. "You need to tell her. Next time I see you...it better be done."

He nodded in agreement. "Since I agree with you, I'll talk to her mother. Sofia is old enough now. She should know the truth. But you're right...she's probably not going to like it."

I shook his hand before I walked out. I headed down the hallway and entered the main lobby of the hotel. But luck wasn't on my side because Sofia must have just returned from lunch. In a tight black dress with matching pumps and a red blazer, she looked fuckable as always.

All I could do was look at her...since touching her was off-limits. My hands slid into the pockets of my slacks as we came closer together.

She stopped in front of me, holding a paper bag. "Just had lunch."

"What did you have?" We were in public, people walking around everywhere.

"A panini."

I'd spent the night last night, and it was so hard to leave. Now, it was hard to stay...to stay and act like she meant nothing to me. My hand wanted to slide into her hair so I could pull her in for a kiss.

"Did you talk to Gustavo?"

"I did. He said he's going to look into it."

"Good. Thank you. I wish he would listen to me that way."

I was a criminal and a murderer, but I wasn't a liar. I hated pretending to be something I wasn't...especially to her. I wanted to come clean because I wasn't ashamed of who I was. I wasn't ashamed of how I earned a living. But I didn't want to scare her off either.

Unfortunately, if I ever wanted there to be a chance to keep her, I had to be straight with her. I couldn't develop her trust with a lie. I couldn't let her think I was someone else...and have feelings for that man instead of me. "Come over for dinner tonight."

If this had been a couple weeks ago, she would have thrown a tantrum on the spot. But our intimacy had deepened, and so did her affection. She still insisted this was a short-term thing, but I was slowly getting her to see me in a different light, to give me a chance to be more than just a fuck buddy. When she smiled, I knew she was about to give me the answer I wanted to hear. "Sure."

THERE WERE several dining tables in the house, but this one had the best view of the city. The top was a long piece of rustic mahogany, big enough to fit twelve grown men. I didn't have meetings at my house often, but I needed something to take up the luxurious space.

Sofia wasn't the kind of woman to talk too much. She didn't need to ramble on to fill the silence, and she didn't take the lack of conversation as an indication of our failed chemistry. She could sit there quietly, switching her gaze between me and her food. "Didn't know you could cook."

Because you don't know anything about me. "I can do everything."

"Everything? That's quite a resume."

We shared a bottle of white wine and picked at our food in silence. Overnight, I'd managed to manipulate this woman into being something she didn't want to be. Now she was having dinner at my house with the intention of sleeping over. Weeks ago, that would have been impossible. I pushed her into a relationship she didn't want to have.

Now I was about to blow it all.

It was enough to make me reconsider my decision. But I shouldn't hide myself from any woman...even if she was the first woman I'd ever wanted. I was proud of the man I was, and I stood by every decision I'd ever made—even pushing a guy out the window. So I looked her in the eye and told her the truth. "I'm the biggest crystal distributor in the south of Europe. My territory includes all of Italy, Greece, and parts of Croatia."

She'd just taken a drink of her wine, and she held her glass there as her throat shifted with the swallow. She slowly lowered it once more, watching me with a guarded expression.

"When I told you I operated a bank, that was the truth. I

opened it years ago, and its main purpose is to launder money for me, as well as my associates."

Her hands came together, and she continued to watch me silently, her green eyes reflecting the light from the suspended chandelier. Her palms gently rubbed past each other as her mind worked to understand everything I had said. "Why are you telling me this?"

"I want you to know who I am." My fingertips rested on the stem of my glass, and I watched her with a rigid posture. She didn't throw the bottle of wine at my head and storm off, so that was a good sign. But her lack of reaction was also concerning. She was either hollow inside...or had the best poker face in the world.

She grabbed her glass and took another drink.

My impatience started to make my fingers twitch.

When she returned it to the table, she licked her lips and looked at her food once more.

I'd lost control of the situation—and it drove me crazy. I had no idea what she was thinking, and that lack of information made my head spin. I couldn't read her...I couldn't feel her. I needed something from her, and it wasn't readily available. "Do you have a problem with that?"

She crossed her arms and leaned against the high-backed chair. "No."

No? She didn't give a damn I was a criminal? "I don't think you understand."

"I'm only interested in you for one reason—so it doesn't matter how you earn your fortune."

Like a bullet to the heart, she pierced me all the way through. It was the most hurtful thing she could have said to me, that I meant so little to her that my job didn't matter. This was going to end anyway—and soon.

"But I think Gustavo has the right to know. Tell him, or I will."

Gustavo hadn't broken the news to her yet. Maybe I should have waited until that conversation was complete. I didn't want to be the one to inform her that her family's legacy was part of a laundering scheme, that it was the site for most business deals in the underworld. All I did was give her a nod.

She grabbed her glass to take another drink.

I should be relieved she wasn't repulsed by me, but I would have preferred that reaction to this indifference. Every woman I'd been with wanted more of me...but Sofia could take me or leave me.

It drove me crazy.

Made me want her more.

"Will I be in danger if I keep seeing you?" Finally, she asked a logical question.

"No one crosses me. I'm also quiet about my private life."

"Not to Damien, apparently."

"He's different. But I don't even tell him about you."

"And why is that?"

Because she was the first woman I actually gave a damn about. I wouldn't describe her perky tits, her tight cunt, the way she swirled her tongue around my dick as she sucked me off. I wouldn't shatter the holiness of our intimacy with gossip. Her scratches, her moans...they all belonged to me. "I'm a very dangerous man. I kill people. Does that bother you?"

"It sounds like you're trying to get rid of me. If that's the case, just be a man and give it to me straight."

That was the last thing I wanted. "It seems like you aren't taking me seriously."

"Who are you killing?"

"People who cross me."

"So criminal men, not innocent people."

I nodded.

"Then it doesn't matter to me." She swirled her wine then took another drink, her tongue swiping across her lips to catch the drops. When there was only a small pool at the bottom of her glass, she set it down and rose to her feet. "I appreciate your honesty, but you don't owe me anything. Just as I don't owe you anything either."

NAILS CUT into my skin as they dragged down my back. Digging deep and leaving scratches behind, they were aggressive...carnal. This woman was white-hot for me, whispering the dirtiest things into my ear. "Yes...fuck me."

I had her pinned underneath me, her tits pressing against my chest as we thrust together. We were both covered in sweat, soiling the sheets with our bodies. I trailed my tongue up her neck so I could taste her saltiness, taste her exertion.

Her fingers dug into my hair, and she moaned.

This woman had been frozen at the dinner table, but now she was a supernova. How could she go from one extreme to the next? How could she feel something then nothing at all? How could I become obsessed with a woman who didn't give a damn about me?

She came around my dick, her eyes looking into mine as she put on a brilliant performance. She arched her back and screamed, my name echoing off the high ceilings of my bedroom.

After a few more pumps, I came inside her, groaning as my body bucked involuntarily. My muscles twitched with completion, and I gave in to the instinctual pleasure. I filled her pussy for the third time, satisfied but also frustrated by this evening.

Just when I thought things were changing between us, she coldly reminded me that I meant nothing to her.

Not a damn thing.

I rolled off her and lay beside her.

She immediately turned away and got comfortable, falling asleep in seconds. Her breathing deepened, and she turned into sleeping beauty on my bed. With her back to me, she had no further use for me.

My job was done.

"You did it." Damien weighed the containers and jotted down the notes.

I ripped off my gloves then shed my protective gear. "Don't act surprised."

"I picked another cook, so you're off the hook." He finished writing down the numbers before he joined me at the sink.

The lab was downstairs in the basement of the building. Only steam evaporated from the building, so no one had any idea crystal was being produced right in the center of the city. I washed my hands then patted them dry. "When can he start?"

"Tomorrow."

"I don't need to train him, right? Because I've got shit to do." I grabbed my jacket off the hook and put it on. My watch was returned to my wrist, and I glanced at the time. I had a large stack of paperwork on my desk waiting for me at the office. This job was never done, so I always had shit to do—maybe that was why I liked it so much.

Damien set the clipboard on the counter. "You alright, man?"

"What the fuck is that supposed to mean?"

He raised his hand and shrugged. "Just seems like you're pissed off about something...more than usual."

I would normally storm out of there without answering him, but my relationship with Sofia was weighing me down, suffocating me. There was a solution to every problem, but with her, there was no quick fix. Unless I kidnapped her and forced her to be mine, I would never really have her.

It was tempting.

"Talk to me." He leaned against the counter next to me, his arm touching mine.

The lab was deserted except for the two of us. The equipment needed to be scrubbed down, and the cleaning crew would be there in a few minutes to do the job. For the moment, we were alone.

"It's about Sofia, isn't it?"

Wow...how far I'd fallen.

"You haven't been the same since you met her. Instead of being in a good mood from all that pussy, you're extra pissed off."

Because she was a pro at pissing me off.

"Talk to me."

We teased each other all the time and were only serious when it came to work. But right now, it was obvious that he was deadly serious, that he wanted to listen to me without casting judgment, that he wanted to help me in whatever way he could. "I told her the truth."

"About this?" he asked, nodding to the equipment we used to make crystal.

"Yeah."

"She didn't take it well?"

"Actually, she did."

"Then I'm not following."

"She's a good girl. She's ambitious, honest, full of integrity... so I assumed she would blow up over this. But since she's just using me, she didn't care at all. She didn't blink an eye over it. She's gonna dump me when she's bored of me, and that will be it. So what does it matter that I'm a drug lord?"

This was the time when Damien would tease me for saying such pussy shit. He would knock me out and hope his punches would beat some sense into me. He would tell me to stop thinking with my dick and start thinking with my goddamn head. But none of that came out of his mouth. "Why did you tell her the truth in the first place?"

"I didn't want to build a relationship on lies."

"But she doesn't want a relationship."

"Now, that's clear, more than ever before..."

"And that bothers you."

It didn't bother me...it drove me fucking crazy.

"Are you in love with her?"

I'd only known her for a month. I didn't know shit about love, but I knew feelings like that built up over a longer period of time. "No." Love was something I'd never encountered, something I'd never considered. Women were all the same—just sexy. But I wanted more than sex with this woman. "But I want to fall in love with her." I said the words out loud, confessing my sins to the priest that was listening.

It was a testament to our friendship when Damien didn't talk shit. "Then keep trying. She'll come around eventually."

"You don't understand...she's ice-cold."

"But she's still sleeping with you—and only you."

I stared at the ground.

"Hades, you never give up on anything. You always get what you want. Why is she any different?"

"Because I've never been in this situation before. Women don't mean a damn thing to me. But the one woman I actually want won't give me the time of day. She just wants my dick—nothing else."

"Then make her want everything else."

I had no idea how to do that.

"Hades, she'll get sucked in so deep, she won't be able to walk away. You have so much power, you could make her never walk away."

I didn't want to force her. I'd never abused my power in that regard, and I wouldn't start now. "No...that's not how I want this to be."

"Then keep trying until she changes her mind. She will change her mind."

He had a lot more faith in my abilities than I realized.

"She'll come around...I know she will."

10

SOFIA

I sat in Gustavo's office and listened to him drop a bomb on me. Everything I believed about my family and its legacy were lies. The Tuscan Rose wasn't a quaint hotel where guests made amazing memories. It was a front for crime.

A front that fooled me.

Gustavo watched me for a minute, anticipating my reaction.

I couldn't think of anything to say, it was so shocking. "I don't believe you..."

My stepfather lowered his gaze and sighed. "I know it's hard to take in...but this is how the real world works."

"No, it's not. There are lots of people out there who earn their living the honest way."

"But anyone who's successful doesn't."

I'd had issues with my father growing up, especially with the way he treated my mother sometimes, but we'd always had a good relationship. He seemed to be ethical, to care about his shiny reputation. It was hard to believe he would be a part of this. "My father wouldn't do that."

"He's the one who started it. It's been going on for decades, Sofia. It doesn't make him a bad man. It doesn't make me a bad man. Not your mother either. It's just how it works."

"So those men who came into the hotel…"

He nodded. "They were men you shouldn't cross. They use our hotel for meetings and drop-offs."

"That man who committed suicide…"

"No, it wasn't a suicide."

I'd been ambitious about taking over this hotel, but it was a circus of crime. Hiding in plain sight, it'd been there all along…I just didn't want to see it. "So, Hades launders your money?" Now I understand what kind of service Hades offered to my family. He was the middle man between Gustavo and the criminals who used the hotel for their own gains. "All those random deposits are from drug dealers and the mafia…"

"Basically."

"The hotel is successful without it. We don't need it, Gustavo."

"Not quite. In the winter months, we're usually barely breaking even. In order to keep all the staff on duty, we need to generate revenue in some other way. This is how it has to be. Since you're so ambitious about taking on this project, I thought you should know. You might want to focus your energy on another career."

Running this hotel, along with the others, had been my dream since I could remember. "These hotels belong to me, Gustavo. What happens when you die? When my mother is gone? I just sell it?"

"No. I'm sure I'll be around a long time, and after you find a suitable partner, he can take over the role."

"I would never marry a man who would want to be part of this operation."

He shrugged. "Then you'll have to sell it."

"And why couldn't I run it myself?" I didn't want to be associated with this kind of deceit, but I also didn't want to be chased away. This was my birthright, an asset I was entitled to. I could always change everything once it was mine, cut ties with all that bullshit my father got mixed up in.

He shook his head slightly. "It's nothing personal, honey. But with these men...it wouldn't be wise."

"I can handle myself." At least long enough to cut ties.

"If that's something you really want, you would need a suitable husband to help you. You would need someone who can do things you can't."

"I can do anything a man can do," I snapped. "And more."

"That's not how I meant it, Sofia. One day, you'll understand."

One day, I would understand that my family was made up of criminals and liars, that they chose to do things the easy way instead of the right way. One day, I would understand that this beautiful hotel was overrun with criminals...including the man I was sleeping with. I was supposed to come to terms with that, just accept it.

Like that would ever happen.

When Hades told me he was a drug dealer, I didn't allow myself to think about it. Just as his customers were addicted to his product, I was addicted to him. My nails were in so deep I never wanted to let go; I didn't want him to slip through my grasp. Ignoring what he said was the only way to accomplish that, to pretend it didn't really happen. I tried not to think about it, to pretend I hadn't heard his confession at all.

Because I wasn't ready to let him go.

I'd finally found exactly what I was looking for, an intense relationship with a man without commitment, something that didn't require a single thought. It was just good sex with a deep connection, something so combustive that I could hardly think about him without my neck getting warm.

I knew there was only one Hades Lombardi in the world, only one man who could fuck like that, could be so damn gorgeous. Once he was gone, it was over. Sex would be mediocre. There would be nothing to look forward to.

Because no man would ever compare.

I SAT in the living room with the TV on, an empty bottle of wine on the table. I'd been drinking all night, my thoughts becoming blurrier with every single glass. I tried to process my emotions, tried to process the reality of my life. Everything I believed in was a lie.

It would take more than a bottle of wine to process that.

My family's legacy was intertwined with criminality. And the man I was sleeping with was a kingpin, apparently.

Maybe I'd always known...deep down inside.

Maybe I was a criminal myself without even realizing it.

A knock sounded on my door.

The TV was on, so I couldn't pretend I wasn't home. I set down my glass then walked to the door. After glancing through the peephole, I realized Hades had dropped by for a visit. He probably knew Gustavo told me the truth. It seemed a strange coincidence that both men came clean about their identities just days apart.

I didn't want to let him into my apartment.

But there was nothing I wanted more than to feel his hand slide into my hair as he kissed me. Feel his strong arms carry me to bed so he could fuck me until we went to sleep. He was my escape from reality, the drug I constantly needed in my veins.

I unlocked the door and let him in.

He was in jeans and a leather jacket, his jawline cleanly shaved. He showed off the masculine structure of his face, the beautiful complexion of his skin. His brown eyes burned into mine the second he looked at me, claiming me right there on the spot.

My hand grabbed the front of his shirt and yanked him into me, bringing our lips together for a passionate kiss in my entryway.

He kicked the door shut behind him and dug his hand into my hair, making me go weak at his touch. He pressed me against the wall and stripped off his jacket.

My hands moved underneath his shirt and touched the warm skin that was heated from his muscles. My fingertips drifted up and felt his hard chest, felt the body I could picture with my eyes closed. This man released endorphins into my brain, gave me such a high that I couldn't quit even if I wanted to. I needed this man to find someone new and forget about me. That way, I would be forced to move on.

He ended the kiss and subtly licked his lips. "You taste like wine."

"You are what you eat, right?" My hands grabbed the bottom of his shirt and slowly peeled it over his body.

He pushed my hands away. "I want to talk."

I pouted my lips and sighed. "Ugh...I hate talking."

"I've noticed." His arms hugged my lower back and placed our foreheads together, holding me in the entryway like he didn't want to talk either. He obviously didn't want to screw either. Otherwise, he would be carrying me down the hallway right now. It seemed like he just wanted to hold me, just feel our beating hearts next to each other.

I was drunk, so any affection was nice. There was nowhere in the world I felt more at ease than when I was in his arms. His kiss made me forget reality, made me forget about all the bullshit in my life.

"Are you alright?"

"I'm fine," I whispered. "Do I not look fine?"

He glanced at the coffee table and noticed the empty bottle sitting next to the remote. "No."

My hands slid down his chest, and I gently pushed him away. "I don't want to talk about it. So, if you want to have sex, that's fine. But if not...then you can just leave." I grabbed the bottle and flipped it over to get any extra drops at the bottom—but it was dry. "Actually, you can take me to pick up another—"

He snatched the bottle out of my hand, along with the glass, and carried it to the sink.

"Wow...I didn't realize drug dealers were so boring."

When he walked back to me, he wore a cold expression on his face, not finding my drunk act very cute. He stopped in front of me, so handsome that I forgot my train of thought. "Baby, be real with me."

"Baby...?"

"Yes." His hand slid into my hair, but he didn't kiss me. He cradled my cheek with his palm, his thumb gently caressing my skin. "Now, talk to me."

"About what?" I whispered. "That my family's legacy is a lie? That everything I believed was just a dream? That one day I'll inherit a corrupt business infested with rats...including you?"

His eyes contracted slightly as he digested that insult.

"The whole reason I went to university was to do this...and now I can't. My father wasn't evil, but he wasn't good either... though I didn't realize how dark he was. I didn't realize my mother has been aware of this since the beginning. I didn't realize this was my life. Even the man I'm sleeping with is a top-tier criminal. It's all around me, and I never noticed… because I didn't want to notice." I lowered my gaze and felt the emotion strike me in the gut.

"The world isn't black-and-white. Not all criminals are evil, and not all law-abiding citizens are good. There's so much gray area there. You've been living in that shade for a long time, so you understand exactly what I mean. Your family may be laundering money and facilitating criminal meetings and the drug trade, but that doesn't make them bad people."

"Wow…that's rich."

His eyes narrowed. "I'm the biggest drug dealer in this part of the world. I get shit done by rewarding those loyal to me and torturing those who aren't. Cross me, and I'll push you out of a goddamn window. Test me, and I'll make you shit your pants. But I stay in my lane and mind my own business. I don't touch innocent people. I don't touch the police. Your family is the same way. The other guys who grow through that hotel have the same agenda. We live in the underworld and don't touch anyone outside of it."

"And none of these men rape and traffic women? You think I'm stupid? I know that's the biggest business out there—"

"I don't do business with those kinds of men. I don't do business with men who do business with those kinds of men." He held my gaze, seeming genuine all the way down to his core. "I kill those kinds of men. Selling drugs or some other product is one thing. But selling a human being is disgusting—especially kids."

His speech shouldn't soften me, but it did. He couldn't be that evil if he actually meant that.

"I've been at war with the Skull Kings for a long time because they practice that bullshit. They stopped a few years ago, and while tensions are still high, I'm not as inclined to fire first...unless they get in my way."

"Who are the Skull Kings?"

"Doesn't matter," he said quickly. "My point is, I'm not a good man...but I'm not evil. When I've paid for sex, it's always with a free woman."

"You've paid for sex?" I blurted. "You're gorgeous. Why would you have to pay for it? That's gross."

His eyes narrowed slightly at the insult, but he didn't strike back. "It's just easier sometimes. I know exactly what I want, and I can pay a woman to be what I want."

I pushed his hands off me. "I'm screwing a man who's screwed prostitutes?"

He let me step back. "Judge me all you want. I'm not ashamed of it."

"Well, you should be. That's disgusting."

"A lot of men do it. If they tell you otherwise, they're lying. At least I have the balls to look you in the eye and say it, even if you're looking back at me with disgust." He held his ground by keeping his strong posture with defiance in his eyes.

I knew so little about the man I was screwing. The more I learned, the less I liked him. That was exactly what I'd feared would happen. I crossed my arms and turned, unsure what my next move was. I was too drunk to think clearly.

"Baby?"

I tried to look away, but I gave in at the tone of his voice.

"I know this is a lot to take in, but after you take some time—"

"Get out."

He held his position, looking at me with the same confidence. He was quiet as he let my command sink in. My hotel was overrun with criminals, and the man I was sleeping with paid for sex. I'd been living in the underworld for so long, and it was my fault for not realizing it. "Get out. Don't come back."

He stayed rooted to the spot, as if he might ignore what I said. He had all the power and I had nothing, so he could do whatever he wanted. I wouldn't be able to stop him. But he bowed his head and headed to the door. He put on his jacket then left without looking back at me.

I was alone, somehow feeling worse now that he was gone. I was chilled to the bone, lonely. He took all the heat in the room and sucked it into his muscular frame, leaving nothing behind. He was bad for me in so many ways, but I was miserable without him. Maybe I'd just been drinking too much, but I was devastated he left. I couldn't think logically with him. I couldn't have a reasonable thought when it came to that man.

Minutes passed, and I knew he would be down by the sidewalk by now. Even if I wanted to catch him, I probably couldn't. But I slipped on my sandals and went after him anyway.

He was standing on the doorstep—as if he knew I would change my mind.

I hated him all over again.

He didn't gloat in victory, didn't crack a smile. His eyes were still full of apology.

Just as I did earlier, I grabbed the front of his shirt and pulled him back inside. Our lips came together like two halves of a whole, and we kissed like that conversation never happened. The door shut, and our clothes dropped to the floor right in the entryway. He lifted me with his strong arms and pinned me against the wall, his cock sliding into my wet pussy like it belonged there.

"Don't leave me…" My fingers dug into his hair, and I kissed him as he thrust inside me, as he hit me so deep, I moaned with every thrust. "I'm not ready."

He ended our kiss so he could look into my eyes. "Never, baby. Never."

I STOPPED WORKING in the office with Gustavo because I wanted nothing to do with the hotel anymore. But I did keep working as a concierge…because I had bills to pay. I stood at the counter and wondered when a shady guy would walk inside, intending to use my hotel for a back-alley meeting.

I was so bitter. I was so foolish.

Stupid.

The large doors to the entryway opened, and a petite woman in a black jacket stepped inside. In designer boots with a ten-thousand-euro handbag, she looked regal. It took me a few seconds to realize this prissy woman was my mother.

I'd been dodging her calls all week.

Her heels echoed off the tile as she came my way, carrying herself like a queen instead of a regular person like everyone else. Black gloves were on her hands, and once she pulled them off, her ridiculous diamond ring was visible. Her ears were adorned with the same luxury, and her clothes reeked of wealth.

I didn't fake a smile. "Checking in?"

She gave that fake smile that drove me crazy. "Honey, how long do you plan to ignore me?"

"Forever."

"That's a long time to be bitter. I suspect I'll outlive you."

"Bitter?" I hissed. "You and Father lied to me...my entire life."

"No. We just decided to tell you when you were old enough. You took an interest in the hotel even when I encouraged you to stay away. Now, you've forced our hand, and we can't protect you any longer. If you had listened to me from the beginning, none of this would have happened."

This wasn't the time or the place for this conversation. Our voices carried easily in the large room, bouncing off the tile walls and the open spaces.

"Let's talk about this later."

"No. You've had plenty of opportunities to name the place and time. We're doing this now."

Bitch.

"Let's have dinner." She pulled on her black gloves once more then tightened her coat.

I didn't want to make a scene in public, so I let her win—this time.

WE WENT to my favorite local place and shared a bottle of wine.

Actually, I hogged it while she had a couple of sips.

Our food arrived at our table, and we still hadn't said a word to each other.

Mother picked up her fork and stirred her pasta around. "I've given you ten minutes to say your piece. Since you haven't spoken a word, I'll talk now."

I stared at her food.

"When your father opened his hotels, he didn't have a lot of money. He needed investors, which is where the board comes from. But even then, it wasn't enough. That was how he began offering special services to special characters."

"And that's never bothered you?"

"No. When I looked at your father, I saw an ambitious man who would do anything to make his dreams come true. I never loved him, but I considered myself very lucky that I got to marry someone with that kind of success."

"You married him for money."

"No," she said with a laugh. "Power. That's why I married him."

This wasn't brand-new information to me, so I didn't judge her for it. Their loveless marriage had a pragmatic beginning. There was tension over the years because things weren't always smooth.

"Power is better than money."

"And you were never worried some of these men might hurt you?"

"No. We've formed an alliance with them. All we do is facilitate a location for them. We're untouchable, and it's been a pleasant experience for nearly thirty years now. If anything, I feel safer knowing exactly where the bad guys are."

"Because they're under your roof," I jabbed.

She placed her fork in her mouth and sucked the pasta off the end. Her mouth moved slowly as she chewed. "I'm sorry you're disappointed, but this is the real world. You either adapt or you die. The partnership has been a very successful one."

"You're breaking the law by laundering money."

"Who doesn't?"

"Lots of people," I snapped.

"But not rich people." She drank her wine.

Was I the only sane person in the world?

"I'm not sure what you want me to say, honey. I'm sorry you're upset, but it's not going to change anything."

"One day, that hotel will be mine."

"And it'll also belong to your husband. You'll choose the right man to handle it."

My eyes narrowed it. "I don't need a man to handle anything—"

"Yes, you do. If you want that hotel, then yes. If you want to go work somewhere else and live a simple life, then no."

"That's ridiculous."

"Those are my terms. It's for your protection. Your father and I agreed on that."

"The man who used to hit you?" I asked coldly.

She stilled at the accusation, like she had no idea I knew that.

When I was growing up, I caught glimpses a few times. He seemed to stop when I got older, probably because he wouldn't be able to hide it anymore. My feelings for him were conflicted, because it seemed like he genuinely loved me and would do anything for me, but he wasn't so kind to others.

She set her fork down on her plate. "I think you're confused—"

"I'm not confused. I distinctly remember you falling to the ground after he punched you. Then he kicked you." I could replay it in my mind so easily...all these years later. There were other moments I could recall, when my parents wouldn't look at each other over dinner, when they would only smile when other people were around. Sometimes, it seemed like they respected each other, even had affection for each other, but it took a very long time for that to happen. Being around other figures in society showed me how fake relationships were, how no one was truly happy.

She stirred her pasta. "We worked through it. He stopped."

"I know he did."

"I wish you hadn't seen that. I don't want you to think badly of your father."

"Too late." I didn't hate him. I just...didn't respect him. I guess I really didn't know him.

"He was a good man. I know that's hard to believe, but he loved you so much. He never loved me, but he adored you."

"I know he did." That much was true.

"So, he wanted to make sure you had the right man to keep you protected. I admire you for being smart and strong-willed, but this is something you can't handle on your own. You need to trust me on that."

"I agree. So, I'll cut ties with all those men and start fresh. I'll run it as a hotel—a real hotel."

Her eyes fell in disappointment. "That won't work either. They won't be happy."

"I'm not running the hotels this way."

"And if you hope to achieve that, you would need a powerful husband to do it. Because they'll laugh in your face and run you off your own property. You still have years to enjoy your youth, so don't worry about it right now."

That was impossible.

"Take some time to process all of this. I'm sure you'll feel differently...eventually."

Unlikely. "That was why you married Gustavo?"

She nodded. "I don't have what it takes to handle men like that. I wanted nothing to do with it, so Gustavo was a good choice. The business keeps running, and I keep being rich. Everyone wins."

Except me. "Just when I think the world can't get bleaker...it does."

"What do you mean?"

"Your first husband beat you until he got help. Your second husband married you so he could run the hotel. Our family's legacy is a con. Everything looks pretty on the outside, but it's so dark on the inside."

"You're looking at it the wrong way, honey," she whispered. "My first husband got help because he hated who he was. My second husband wants to protect me and my wealth. My hotel is flourishing, giving us the life your father would have wanted us to have. Everything changes based on your perspective...so get the right perspective."

Tuscan Rose was hosting a formal dinner for all the local businesses in the area, notably those who contributed to the hotel in some way. Running an establishment like that created lots of relationships, some better than others.

Damien and I were attending. I wasn't sure if Sofia was. She was upset with her mother and stepfather for their approach to running the hotel, and since she was a sassy little thing, her attitude wouldn't die out easily.

"She gonna be there?" Damien asked as he drove the Ferrari down the narrow streets.

"Don't know."

"You didn't ask?"

"I assume she's not. Probably would have mentioned it if she were."

"And you didn't mention it to her?" he asked in surprise.

"It's a sore subject…"

He turned down the street then approached the valet in front of the hotel. "You think there will be pussy at this thing?"

"There's pussy everywhere, Damien."

"Then maybe we should have driven separately."

"I can get myself home if you're so lucky." The valet took the car, and we walked inside. We made it to the top floor, the same exact place where Sofia and I met for the first time. When I saw hundreds of people crowded into the ballroom, nostalgia hit me and I was taken back to four years ago, when Sofia was barely legal. It was a cold night just like this, and people were so absorbed in conversation, they didn't notice the young couple slip outside.

Damien took a look around, his hands in his pockets. "This looks like a snooze-fest to me."

"What are you expecting? Strippers?"

He snapped his fingers. "Now that would be awesome."

A waitress came over and offered us champagne.

Damien took a glass then stared at her ass as she walked through the crowd.

A flashback of our time in Morocco came back to me. We'd been walking through the bazaar when a group of pretty girls passed, and Damien immediately turned to watch them, making an identical expression to the one he did now.

I'd been thinking about that night a lot recently, that purple tent with the gold vases in the corner. The gypsy wore a blue-eyed pendant from her necklace, as if that was the source of her all-seeing power. I'd been just a boy at the time, turning twenty-one and so hard up that I spent all my cash at the brothel. When she read my future, I didn't care so much about the results. But my feelings for Sofia were only growing...and the height of her walls never changed. That prophecy couldn't be true, right?

"How about you do the mingling?" Damien asked. "There is one fine piece of ass sitting all alone. I should go over there and ruin her night." He handed his half-finished glass to me like I was the help.

"Could you act professional for once in your life?"

"I'm a drug dealer." He said it with a grin, like he didn't care who overheard him. "I'm definitely not professional."

Thankfully, another waiter passed with an empty tray, so I placed his glass on top.

I moved through the crowd and made small talk with a few people I knew. My eyes scanned for Gustavo and his step-daughter, whom I eventually found.

In a red dress with a high slit, she stood in five-inch black pumps. Her back was turned to me, but I recognized that deep brown hair anywhere. So thick and easy to fist. Her hourglass figure was noticeable too, especially since it made me hard in my slacks. She stood beside her stepfather and spoke to another man in a suit, someone else associated with the hotel.

My eyes fell to the petite woman beside her. She had similar features and the same green eyes, and I knew that was her mother. I'd seen her before, but it'd been so long that I probably wouldn't have recognized her. She aged with immortality, somehow defying wrinkles and keeping her complexion beautiful. She was still exceptionally slender, taking care of her figure like she might hit the runway soon.

I understood where Sofia got her looks from.

I swam through the crowd, slowly making my way toward them so I could get a better look at her. When I faced her direction, I got to see her full appearance, see that curled hair pushed back over her shoulders to show off her beautiful face. Red lipstick outlined those plump lips, and the dark shadow around her eyes gave them a smoky look. She was the Tuscan Rose, the red flower that always bloomed.

I stared at her for a long time, enjoying my vantage point. She hadn't noticed me yet, so I soaked in the look of her sexy curves, the way her dress fit snugly over her chest. A cleavage line was noticeable because her tits were pressed firmly together.

My hard dick was never going to rest until I was deep inside her.

She and her family seemed to be busy talking to people, so I approached them with my hand extended to Gustavo. "Beautiful party."

Sofia's eyes moved to my face, her previous look of boredom quickly replaced by a mixture of arousal and fear. If we were alone together, she would probably grab the front of my shirt and yank me into her.

I loved it when she did that...like I was hers to push around.

"Thank you," Gustavo said. "This is my wife, Maria. I'm sure you've met in the past, but it's been a long time."

I shook hands with her mother, giving her a polite smile. "I remember you very well. Beautiful as ever."

She smiled back, the affection reaching her eyes. "Well, thank you."

I turned to Sofia next. A handshake seemed odd when we were intense lovers. Anytime I touched her hand, I was usually pinning it behind her back or against the mattress. A cordial smile didn't seem right, not when we hardly ever smiled at each other. I was used to watching her come, her mouth gaping open and tears leaking from the corners of her eyes. "It's always a pleasure to see you, Sofia." I leaned in and kissed her on the cheek.

Stunned by my forwardness, she remained still.

I turned back to her family like nothing happened. "Enjoy your evening."

12

SOFIA

MOTHER WALKED BESIDE ME, A DRINK IN HER HAND. "SO, WHY didn't you bring that man you're seeing?"

"Because we aren't serious."

"You've been sleeping with him for a long time. Seems serious."

I stopped in my tracks and looked at her. "I like it better when you're my mother, not my friend."

She brushed off the insult by stirring her olive in her glass. "I'm just looking out for you."

"How is asking about my sex life looking out for me?"

"Because Hades Lombardi seems smitten with you."

Of course he does...because he didn't even bother hiding it. He eye-fucked me right in front of my mother like he didn't give a damn. "He's not my type."

"Really?" she asked. "Because Gustavo says he's made quite a name for himself. He's self-made. Started his own bank in his twenties. That's impressive. Not to mention, he's tall, extremely handsome, polite."

That man was definitely not polite. "I'm not interested."

"Then are you sleeping with a woman?" She grabbed my arm and pivoted my body so I would be forced to look at him across the room. "There are at least three women staring at him as we speak."

There were more than three. "Just leave it alone, alright?"

"He would probably make a good husband."

I rolled my eyes. "You don't even know him."

"No, but I know men...and he's into you."

I had to give her credit for that.

"I'm gonna go mingle. Just think about what I said." She clinked her glass against mine then walked away.

I was lonely in the crowd, staring at the man who secretly occupied my bed. I watched as a beautiful woman in a black dress approached him and talked to him for a while. Jealousy rose in my chest like a tiger about to pounce, but I reminded myself he wasn't mine. He would never be mine. He was just a good memory to cherish later.

They talked for a little while longer before she excused herself from the conversation.

I wondered if she'd asked him out, but he said no.

"This party could use some strippers and club music. The quartet is so overrated." Damien appeared beside me, wearing a black suit with a matching tie. In his hand was a glass of scotch—on the rocks. His body was aligned with mine so we were both looking at Hades across the room.

Hades stood near the wall in the corner, his eyes moving to mine like I was a target. He drank from his glass as he watched me, never dropping his gaze. He was the hunter, and I was the hunted.

Damien gave me a gentle nudge in the side. "Are you gonna make him stand there alone all night?"

"He doesn't have to stand alone if he doesn't want to."

"He wants to be alone...unless you're there with him." He moved into my line of sight and faced me head on. He had dark hair and a shadow on his face, but his charm was boyish. He had a dimple in each cheek, a playful sheen in his eyes. "Every woman in this room would kill to go home with him. You've hit the jackpot, and you don't even know it."

"Drug dealers are jackpots now?" I asked sarcastically.

Once he heard the subtle insult, he turned serious. "A man who can control territory the way he does is a fucking powerhouse. He's the most brilliant guy I've ever met, and based on all the broken hearts he leaves behind, he's the best at a lot of things." He took a drink then walked away, letting me chew on that final message.

I handed my drink to a passing waiter and made my way over to Hades. My mother was busy talking to some of her friends, and Gustavo was so overwhelmed by guests that I was the last thing on his mind.

Hades kept watching me as I came near, his eyes growing more intense the closer I got. He looked my figure up and down with heated eyes, like he wanted to hike up my dress and fuck me against the wall.

When I reached him, I took the glass out of his hand and took a drink.

Scotch. Cliché.

He watched me drink, his hand sliding into his pockets.

I finished the whole thing and set the empty glass on a nearby table.

"What did Damien say to you?"

"Not much." I looked into that handsome face and grew weak like always. My fingers tightened into a fist automatically because I wanted to grab him and pull him into me, planting a kiss on those scotch-soaked lips. "Just that you have a big dick and I should be sucking it right now."

A slow grin subtly moved onto his lips. "I don't disagree with that."

"You want me to get on my knees right now and suck you off?"

The playfulness in his eyes died away immediately. He slowly morphed into the intimidating man I met a long time ago. His body oozed confidence, his eyes burning with possessiveness. "I wouldn't stop you." He moved toward me, coming so close that if anyone were watching, they would know we'd seen each other naked so many times. His chin tilted down toward my face, and he leaned in and pressed a gentle kiss to my lips.

I didn't stop him.

He pulled away and watched my expression. "I'm about to dig my hand into your pretty hair and kiss you so good, you come on the spot. We both know I don't give a shit who sees us. They can watch me fuck you for all I care. So, don't play games with me. You'll lose—I promise you."

"I wasn't playing games." My hand slid up his stomach to his chest, and my fingers dug into the fabric of his collared shirt. I gave it a gentle tug, stretching the premium cotton. I didn't tug him into me for a kiss. Instead, I let him go then rubbed my hand over the defined bulge in his slacks.

I stepped away and moved to the balcony. The doors were closed because it was too cold on this winter night to move the party outside. I stepped onto the terrace then moved to the side of the patio, the place where I'd kissed him for the first time.

He followed behind me.

This time, I pushed him against the wall before I moved in and kissed him. I rose on my tiptoes and kissed his eager mouth, feeling his hand slide into my hair as he pulled me close. If anyone looked out the window, they might be able to see our dark figures moving around, but it would be hard to make out.

My fingers got his slacks open, and I pushed them down over his hips slightly, getting his cock free.

Then I lifted up my dress and got down on my knees.

His eyes narrowed in surprise as he looked down at me, his fat cock exposed to the cold air. His body tightened as his hand moved into my hair again, and he guided my mouth to his length.

Once I pushed my throat over his hard dick, he moaned like it was the first time he'd had a wet mouth around his cock. "Jesus…"

I opened my mouth as wide as I could and lifted my gaze to meet his. Then I sucked his dick hard and fast, proving I wasn't the least bit scared either. He had a big dick, so he took up my entire throat with his girth. It made it hard to breathe, impossible to swallow, and my eyes stung with tears.

He thrust his hips and dug deep inside me, pushing that fat cock as far as he could go because he knew I could handle it. His hand wrapped around my hair like a lasso, getting a controlling grip that kept me in place.

Not that I was going anywhere.

I liked his dick in my mouth. I liked pleasing him. I liked surprising him. He was the one who liked to be in control all the time, so it was sexy to see him vulnerable, for him to let me do whatever I wanted so he could enjoy it.

When his dick hardened in my mouth like he was about to come, he pulled my eager mouth off his dick. "Up." He dragged me by the arm and pulled me to my feet before he pressed me against the wall. My dress was yanked up, my panties were pulled to the side, and he wrapped my leg around his waist so he could fuck me.

He slid inside me easily, soaked in my spit.

I moaned because his cock always felt so good, especially after I sucked it off.

He pressed me against the wall and rested his face against mine, supporting me as he worked his hips to push deep inside me over and over. He breathed against my mouth, his desire audible.

My fingers dug into his hair as I held him close, as I let him smother me into the wall to keep me warm. Four years ago, I'd wanted to be just like this, letting this beautiful man fuck me. But it never would have been as good then as it was now.

His hips slowed down, and he moved his mouth to mine to kiss me. His embrace was gentle, full of purposeful kisses and deep breaths. That was when everything started to move in slow motion. Seconds ago, we were yanking on each other in desperation. Now, we wanted to take our time, like we were home in bed. He wanted to make this last, commit this moment to memory.

I deepened the kiss as our bodies moved together on that rooftop, as we clung to each other in the cold air. The skin of my back and shoulders shivered when it came into contact with the cold stone, but now I was so hot, I was working up a sweat. "What if someone sees...?" We'd been gone from the party a long time, and my mother shrewdly noticed everything. She would probably figure out that Hades absent from the party as well.

He pulled the string at the nape of my neck and let my dress fall forward, let my tits become exposed to the nighttime air. His big dick sank inside me over and over, and he crowded me farther into the wall as he fucked me good and slow. "Let them see."

13

HADES

In a daze, I sat alone at a table as the party wound down. Couples had been departing over the last hour, and the people who stayed behind were taking forever to say goodbye. Alone, I enjoyed my drink as I replayed what had just happened on that balcony.

This woman was going to kill me.

I was the kingpin of the drug world, selling the purest stuff on the market, but not once had I taken a hit. That shit messed people up for a long time, so I didn't get involved in that lifestyle. My two vices were cigars and booze. Pussy too, if that counted. But Sofia was my drug, the addiction I couldn't break...not that I was trying. When we were wrapped together, it was the closest to heaven I would ever be. When my time on earth was over, I would be sent to hell on the expressway.

At least I'd gotten to touch an angel before I left.

Damien fell into the chair beside me and set his valet ticket on the tablecloth. "Take the car."

"You've got other plans?" I shoved the ticket into my pocket.

"That waitress lives down the block. I'm gonna walk her home."

"It's freezing outside."

"Yeah, but I'm sure her cunt is nice and warm." He nudged me in the side then nodded his head in her direction. "She's got one hell of an ass."

I glanced at her but wasn't impressed by what I saw. I'd never been picky when it came to women, but Sofia ruined all other women for me. They had nothing compared to her gorgeous face, sexy legs, and pussy made of crystal. "Have fun."

"What are you gonna do?"

Go home with my woman. Just not sure how I was gonna pull that off. "Not sure."

He glanced at Sofia across the room. "I talked you up to her."

"She told me."

"Hoped it helped."

"It did." Big time.

"I'll admit she's an exceptionally beautiful woman, but what's your fascination with her? You can have any woman you want, and she'll want you back. But you seem to like the one woman who doesn't. Is that why you're obsessed with her? Because you can't have her?"

I had no idea why I felt this way. All I knew was I didn't want anyone else but her. "I'm not sure. If I ever figure it out, I'll let you know."

He clapped me on the back and rose to his feet. "I'll see you later, man."

"Night."

He walked away and picked up the waitress. They walked off together.

My eyes moved back to the woman who'd stolen my obsession. A young man was talking to her now, probably lingering behind so he could have the opportunity to ask her out. He was a good-looking guy but nowhere near her caliber.

I could be jealous, but I wasn't.

Real men don't get jealous.

She must have turned him down because he walked away empty-handed.

I HANDED the ticket to the valet outside so they could retrieve the car.

Sofia and her family entered the lobby a moment later, their coats protecting them from the cold they would have to feel once they walked outside. Even with her body encased in enough fabric to hide her curves from sight, her legs were enough to make mouths drop.

Maria spotted me, and a spark of mischief came into her

eyes. She broke away from her husband and walked up to me. "Heading home?"

"Yes. It was a lovely evening. Thank you for the invitation." I leaned in and kissed her on the cheek.

She turned her face, giving me good exposure. "We're very happy that you attended."

The Ferrari pulled up to the curb. "Have a good night."

"Hades." Her slender fingers gently wrapped around my arm. "Gustavo and I will be here a little longer. Would you mind taking my daughter home?" She turned to her daughter. "Honey, come here."

It looked like I had her mother's approval. She was playing matchmaker right in front of my eyes.

Sofia turned to us, clearly uncomfortable at the sight of us talking. She joined us, rigid and cold in her mother's presence. The heat we'd shared on the balcony was long gone because her resentment overshadowed everything.

"Hades is going to take you home," Maria said. "We'll be here awhile longer, and I don't want you to wait around."

"I can walk." That was Sofia's preferred method of transportation...even though it pissed me off.

Maria laughed it off, but her eyes showed her embarrassment. "You're funny, honey. Good night." Once she put the two of us together, she walked away so the magic between us could spark.

Even though we were already two explosive volcanoes.

I extended my arm to her. "Let's go."

Sofia was still annoyed, so she didn't take my arm. She walked forward and stepped into the nighttime air, holding her head high like a queen.

I opened the door for her then got behind the wheel. I turned up the heat before I drove away.

She looked out the window. "Is this your car?"

"Damien's."

"And where is he?"

"Getting blown."

She smiled slightly and pulled her coat tighter around her.

"Your mother seems to like me." My line of business wouldn't be a problem for us like it would for most people. Maria had a realistic view of the world. She understood I was powerful enough to remain invincible in my work, so obviously, I could protect her daughter. I could provide for her. I could keep that hotel running smoothly and protect the Romano family.

"Don't take it as a compliment."

"Hard not to. It's difficult to earn the approval of the mother."

"You don't need her approval."

No, but it would be much easier.

"Besides, I'm not sure how much she would like you if she knew what we did on the balcony."

"Seems to me that's exactly what she wants."

She turned her head back toward the window, dismissing the conversation.

I could feel her negative energy, feel her anger heat up the car.

"You shouldn't be so hard on her."

She snapped. "Don't tell me how to feel about my own family. You think you know everything, but you know nothing."

She'd never really confided in me about anything. Everything I'd gathered about her was through observation. She was an honest person who strived for greatness, and she had an attitude while she did it. She was different from the rest of us because she still possessed her moral compass. But she didn't understand the real world didn't play by the rules. It played for survival.

I approached her building.

"Just drop me off here, and I'll walk up."

I wasn't giving up that easily. "I'm walking you to your door."

"I don't need you to walk me to my door."

I ignored her and parked.

When she didn't get what she wanted, she sighed and shoved the door open.

I followed behind her and walked up the stairs until we arrived at her door.

She unlocked the door and stepped inside without looking at me, shutting the door in my face.

I steadied it with my hand and invited myself inside.

"I just want to be alone—"

My hand slid into her hair, and I kissed her. My arm hugged her waist, and I pulled her close, heating her up after the frozen walk to her apartment. I gently guided her against the wall, to the place where I'd fucked her the last time I was here.

She kissed me back, slightly timid because of her previous rage.

I pulled away and locked the door behind me. My jacket slid down my arms before I hung it on the coatrack. My tie joined it.

She watched me. "You're presumptuous."

"I know." I kicked off my shoes and unbuttoned my collared shirt, getting the layers off my body until I was just in my slacks.

She finally took off her coat and left her heels by the door. She was still in a foul mood, so it didn't seem like sex was on the menu tonight. Truth be told, I didn't come there to be inside her.

I just wanted to talk to her.

What kind of man was I? That wasn't me.

She grabbed a bottle of wine and uncorked it.

Instead of snatching it away, I let her be.

She set two glasses on the dining table and filled them to the brim. She sat in her red dress and took a deep drink, handling it like juice instead of alcohol.

She was the most complex person I'd ever met. "What don't I know?"

She cocked her head slightly.

"Tell me."

"Honestly, the last thing I want to do is talk about my family. I never ask you about yours."

"It wouldn't bother me if you did." She never asked anything remotely personal, trying to keep this arrangement as sterile as possible. In her defense, she'd told me what she wanted on day one. It was the same behavior I directed toward tons of women. I wasn't playing hard to get; I was just being honest so they wouldn't expect anything more out of me. Now the roles had reversed...and I was infatuated with a woman who didn't give a damn about me. Maybe it was karma. "I know all of this has been a big pill to swallow. Enormous. But as you get older, you start to realize that life isn't fair, that no one plays by the rules, that the most honorable people are liars. Your family has done what was necessary to survive. You should never apologize for what you have to do to support your family."

She stared at me coldly.

"Your comment about my relationship with prostitutes is unfair. Prostitution is the oldest profession in the world. They do what's necessary to survive—"

"You misunderstood me. I don't judge women for being whores or strippers. They can do whatever they want. I was just caught off guard when you admitted you use their services. You're so goddamn beautiful that you can have any woman you want. Why would you need to pay for it? And secondly, I'm not living in a fairy tale. I understand the difference between good and evil is separated by miles of gray area. No one is completely good, because if they were, they wouldn't be good. My issue is, everything I'd been told is bullshit. Nothing is real. Acclimating to that has been difficult. I'm not some stuck-up brat who needs to get her way. It's just painful to learn that the one good thing about your late father is a lie. So he was never good...he was always bad."

I held on to my glass as I stared at her, afraid to say anything because it might spook her. She was finally giving me insight into her world, finally showing me who she was.

"My mother told me I have to marry a powerful man for the family. If I ever want that hotel business, it's a requirement. Watching her manipulate my life like that, playing cupid and pulling on invisible strings like I'm a puppet...is sickening. You're the only man I want, but watching her push you on me makes me want you less."

I focused on the key part of that sentence...*you're the only man I want.*

"I've wanted the family business since I was young, and now being told I'll never be good enough is insulting. It doesn't matter how good I am. I'll never be worthy."

"That's not true."

Her eyes narrowed.

"You can run that hotel all on your own. You just need the world to know that a very powerful man will make heads roll if they cross you. It's like a personal security system, a bodyguard. You're taking it the wrong way."

She brought her glass to her lips to take a drink. "If I ever get that hotel, I want to disband all of those criminal arrangements and run it the right way."

That wouldn't be wise, but since it was so far into the future, I didn't bother arguing with it. "I'm sure your mother is a lot to handle, but at the end of the day, she's just looking out for you. She's in your corner."

She drank her wine again.

"Why was your father a bad man?"

"They're both bad—my mother and father."

"And why is that?"

"For one, my mother has so little faith in herself that she signs her soul over to whatever man will take her. Her lack of independence is troubling. She stands in his shadow and never allows herself to shine. And my father..." Her eyes glazed over as she considered what she was about to say.

I stayed patient, needing that answer like I needed air.

"He was good to me. I always knew he loved me. But in my younger years, he used to beat my mother...pretty badly."

In a single moment, the clouds parted and the horizon became so clear.

"It went on for a long time until she somehow convinced him to stop. But I still remember the way he punched her to the floor and kicked her ribs in. They thought I never knew about it since it's a big house...but I knew."

She didn't need to explain much else. Now I understood her perfectly. She didn't trust men—especially not me. Her whole life, she'd witnessed loveless marriages, artificial commitments, and being caged. Her mother was a slave to her husband, repeatedly marrying for protection but getting hurt in the process. Sofia had no faith in the institution... and she certainly had no faith in love.

As punishment for your crimes, you will only love one woman...but she'll never love you back.

I pushed away the thought. "I'm sorry."

She swirled her wine before she took a drink. Her lipstick smeared on the glass, leaving an imprint of her plump lips.

"But not all men are like that. Not all relationships are like that."

"I used to think the same thing. But now that I know the truth about the hotel...about the people I've known my entire life, I realize it is true. There's no escaping it. This is hell...and we're all living in the underworld."

I WOKE up the following morning with a beautiful woman all over me. Her face was pressed into the crook of my neck, and her arm was hooked around my waist. One leg was tucked between mine, and her hair was all over the place.

I remained still because I wanted to stay like this forever.

Her smell washed over me, rosy perfume and sex. Her hair was soft to my fingertips even though it was dry from the hairspray. Her curls had come loose from rolling around last night.

I woke up with morning wood, but seeing her snuggled into my side only made me harder.

Her bed wasn't nearly as comfortable as mine, but I'd rather be there with her than alone at home—or worse, with someone else. I could pay a woman to fuck me exactly how I wanted, but it wasn't as good as what we had. When I fucked Sofia, I gave everything I had, my heart, soul, and body. I didn't hold anything back, letting all the pieces of me mix in with her. Every time she hurt me, I only wanted to try harder, to fix her broken outlook on the world.

But now I feared she could never be fixed. Her pessimistic perspective was solidified in her bones like cement. She craved freedom more than commitment, wanted the ability to stay or leave whenever she wanted. The last thing she wanted was a man, because they were a liability, not an asset.

This was the best it would ever get.

She opened her eyes minutes later, stretching her legs and taking a deep breath as the morning washed over her. Her arm hugged my waist a little tighter, and she pressed a kiss to my chest, her lipstick gone because I'd kissed it away last night.

She was gorgeous first thing in the morning.

She sat up then straddled my hips, her eyes still heavy with sleep. She pointed my dick to her tight entrance than slowly sank down, gradually stretching her body apart with my intrusion. She moaned once he was completely in, and she started to grind.

I held on to her hips and watched her fuck me, watched her

enjoy me without shame. She took what she wanted without apology.

That was exactly how I liked her.

She finished us both off then got out of bed like nothing happened. She fished a shirt out of her drawer then walked down the hallway.

I almost stayed behind because I was satisfied, getting the best sex of my life without having to lift a finger. But I pulled on my boxers and followed her into the kitchen.

She already had a bowl of cereal in front of her, and she was texting on her phone. Her feet were pulled to her chest at the dinner table, her ankles crossed.

I sat across from her and ran my fingers through my hair.

She set her phone down. "I'm going shopping with Esme." She didn't even finish her cereal because her plans were more important. "I need to get in the shower. Let yourself out." She walked past me.

Every time we moved a few steps forward, she abruptly turned in the opposite direction and hit the gas. Whenever she felt anything meaningful, she shut it down and pretended it never happened.

I grabbed her by the arm and dragged her back toward me. I forced her into my lap, our eyes locked on to each other. "I'm your man, alright? So, stop treating me like a stranger you picked up last night. Stop cooling us off the second we get hot. I know exactly what you're doing, so knock it off."

She stayed quiet, put on the spot like a deer in the headlights.

"I would never hurt you."

She dropped her gaze altogether.

I squeezed her arm and gave a gentle tug. "Look at me."

Her eyes shifted back to me.

"I promise you." I grabbed her hand and placed it over my slow-beating heart. "I'm the kind of man that keeps his promises, so I hardly ever make them. I'm true to my word. There are a lot of assholes out there, but I'm not one of them. I'm the kind of man that would rather die than let something happen to you. I'm the kind of man that will rip apart a man who even looks at you wrong. I'm the kind of man that gives everything when he's committed to some-thing. If I were committed to you…I would never let you down." A speech like that had never left my lips in my entire life. I hardly gave a woman a few minutes of my time once the sex was over, but here I was, fighting for just seconds of her attention. I'd never worked so hard for anything in my life, but I was pouring my heart out to her just for the chance to actually have her. Every time she turned me down, it was like a knife to the heart. It really did feel like a punishment, like someone out there put a curse on me. "Baby, give me a chance." I'd never wanted something so much in my life, something that made my hands shake when the rest of my body was absolutely still.

Her hand slid away from my heart, and she rose to her feet.

I already knew what she was going to say. My heart tight-ened in preparation for the rush of pain, the torture I was about to feel.

She moved behind me so she wouldn't have to look at me. "I don't think we should see each other anymore."

THE VEHICLES PULLED up to the farmhouse, driving through the white picket fence around the property even though the road would have been just as easy to take. My gun was shoved into the back of my jeans, and I ditched my jacket because my temperature was running high.

Once we were on the grass, I hopped out and headed to the front door.

Damien lingered behind, letting me take the lead.

I kicked down the front door to the sound of screams.

A woman picked up her young son and sprinted away from me. Another kid cried from a different part of the house.

His voice was audible. "Stay behind me."

I rounded the corner and saw Miles standing in front of his family, keeping his arms back so his wife and his two kids were protected. A gun was on his hip, but the second he saw the vehicles storm his property, he knew it was pointless. His wife sobbed as she held her two kids close to her chest.

His chest exploded with every breath, and a film of moisture covered his eyes with emotion. "Please don't hurt them... please." His bottom lip shook, his emotion uncontrollable. "I know you're here for me, not them. Please, let them go."

His wife was beautiful, so any other man would rape her right in front of him and shoot his kids. Luckily for him, that wasn't me. "Come with me."

He stayed with his family as if he didn't know what else to do.

"Make this easy, and I'll spare them."

Miles dropped his arms and slowly stepped away.

"No!" His wife tried to grab his arm. "Please don't kill my husband...please."

Miles didn't look at her, as if one final look would be too much.

I grabbed him by the arm and dragged him to the front of the house, ignoring their loud screams. The rest of my men moved in and secured the perimeter. I dragged Miles to the front of the house and shoved him onto the lawn.

Damien was there, looking at Miles with disgust.

I lifted my pistol and aimed at his forehead. "Kneel."

Miles raised his arms and slowly moved to the ground.

I stepped forward, bringing the gun closer. "Your brother killed my best cook. I'm sure you know that."

He gave a slight nod.

"So what do you think is going to happen to you?"

His entire body shook as he avoided looking at the gun. He wanted me to pull the trigger when he didn't know it was coming, to end his life mercifully.

I wasn't a merciful guy—and I was fucking pissed off.

"Give me your phone."

Miles reached into his pocket and withdrew it.

Damien grabbed it and called Maddox, putting it on speakerphone.

It was almost dusk, and the cold wind had a serious bite. It stung our skin as it blew through the countryside. The phone continued to ring until that asshole finally picked up. "Miles, how's the family?"

Miles stayed quiet.

I spoke into the phone, my aim steady. "Let me paint a picture for you. I've got your brother on his knees, a gun pointed to his head, and his wife and kids are sobbing inside the house. It's time to even the score."

Maddox was silent.

"You killed my best cook, and now I'll kill your best brother. Does that sound even?"

More silence.

"Lucky for you, I'm just as good a diplomat as I am a killer. Get the fuck out of my territory and disappear, and your brother lives. If you don't honor your word, then I'll kill him and his family next time."

Miles visibly relaxed, knowing his brother would agree to the terms and spare his life.

Maddox was still quiet, debating my offer. There was no way around the situation. He either had to cave or lose his brother...or live with the blood on his hands. He finally came to a decision. "No."

Miles took a deep breath.

"No deal," Maddox said. "Do what you have to do." He hung up.

Miles lowered his head and started to hyperventilate. He had just been betrayed, his life inferior to the territory his brother wanted to conquer. In his last moments of life, he felt like nothing...nothing at all.

I almost felt so badly for him that I didn't pull the trigger. But now Maddox turned the tables, and if I didn't make good on my word, he would never take me seriously ever again. Word would spread that I was a pussy, and I couldn't have that.

"I'm sorry." I pulled the trigger.

The gunshot echoed across the countryside with a loud explosion.

Then sobs started from the house once more.

I holstered my gun and looked away from his dead body. "Bury him." I normally wouldn't bother, but I didn't want his wife to see him like this. It wasn't right.

The men got to work and dug a hole.

Screams came from the house, but they weren't screams of pain, they were screams of terror.

I entered the house and found his wife pinned down, the kids in the corner as they watched in horror. Two of my men were undressing her.

"Get off her. Now."

Both men obeyed.

I'd shoot them right then and there, but it wasn't the place. "Outside."

They left the house.

The woman yanked her clothes back on then returned to her children, shielding them with her body. She wouldn't look at me as she trembled, traumatized by everything that had happened. She was scarred for her life…so were her children.

I walked back outside and found the men who'd taken matters into their own hands.

I killed them both. "Leave them."

I got back into the vehicle with Damien and left the property. We drove down the dirt road until we reached the main highway. Then we began the quiet journey home. I hadn't accomplished what I set out to do, but I had established Maddox's mind-set. Overrunning me was his primary goal —and he wouldn't stop for anything.

Not even family.

I turned to Damien, the man I considered to be a brother. We'd known each other forever, had been side by side through thick and thin. Everything I worked for was important, but never more important than him. "I'd rather lose everything than lose you."

His eyes softened, and he gave a slight nod. "Me too."

I sat on the balcony in my sweatpants, not minding the cold air as it hit my bare chest. Helena made me Indian cuisine for dinner, butter chicken with jasmine rice and naan. I took a few bites then let it get cold.

My mind was miles away as I watched the cars drive down the narrow streets, listened to the bells toll from the Catholic church a few blocks away. It was a clear night so the stars were visible, but the lack of clouds made it colder than usual.

I should be out drinking or fucking, but I was here...alone.

I'd left Sofia's apartment a week ago and never returned. I didn't text or show up on her doorstep. She dumped me, and I had too much respect for myself to chase after her. She was too scared to let me in, but that was her problem.

Even though I missed her like crazy.

Helena knocked on the bedroom door before she came inside. "How was dinner?" She picked up the plate and utensils and shook her head slightly. "Not very good, I take it." With fair skin and blond hair, she also had a Swedish accent.

"I just don't have much of an appetite."

"Not for food, at least." She glanced at the nearly empty bottle of scotch. "Damien is here to see you. Shall I send him up?"

"Why is he here?"

"No idea. Getting answers from him is like pulling teeth." She stepped inside and carried the dirty dishes with her. "I'll send him up."

I looked at the city once more, suffocated by all the shit in my life. Maddox was becoming a worse enemy than I realized, and I still felt guilty for killing his brother. That plan backfired in my face because I assumed Maddox would cave. When he didn't, I had to make Miles's wife a widow.

I was a fucking monster.

Damien stepped onto the patio in a long-sleeved shirt and a jacket. "It's fucking freezing. Why are you sitting out here like that?" He fell into the chair opposite me, helping himself to the booze on the table. "Trying to catch a cold?"

"I don't get sick."

"Alright...trying to freeze to death?"

"I'm never cold." My fingertips rested against my lips, and I looked at the city.

Damien let the booze wash down his throat. "You've been moody all week. What's up? Are you still pissed about the Maddox thing? Don't worry, we'll get that asshole."

"No."

"Then what's got you so bitchy?"

I rubbed my fingertips against my temple, hating myself for allowing a woman to ruin me like this. I was busting my ass for a woman who didn't give a damn about me. Fucking pathetic. Most women would do anything to earn my affection, but Sofia tossed it away like garbage. How had I let things get so bad?

"You aren't getting laid?"

"Actually, no." It would be easy for me to pick up a piece of ass, even pay for it, but the thought never crossed my mind.

I was loyal to a woman who wasn't even mine. She'd turned me into a pussy-whipped dumbass.

He cocked an eyebrow. "What happened with Sofia?"

"She dumped me." I'd never been dropped by a woman so easily. Normally, I couldn't get them to leave me the hell alone. But she kicked me to the curb like an afterthought.

"Seriously?"

I nodded.

"When?"

"A week ago."

"Did she say why?"

It was all my fault. I'd pushed too fast. I wasn't even sure what came over me. I just wanted her to drop her attitude and open up a bit. "I rushed it."

"Did you tell her you love her or something...?"

"No. I just... I'm just trying too hard."

"So, she broke it off with you."

I nodded. "Her stance on a relationship hasn't changed since we met. She wants sex...nothing else."

"That sounds perfect. Why don't you just leave it alone?"

"Because...I just can't." I would never admit this out loud to anyone but Damien. It made me so weak, made me laughable. This woman had broken my heart, and I hadn't even given it to her yet. We'd been screwing for a relatively short amount of time, but I felt like I'd lost a piece of me. We hadn't even talked about anything serious, and she hardly knew me. But I felt like I knew her...so damn well.

"If you're this miserable, why don't you try to get her back?"

"Because I have too much pride. I'm not gonna chase a woman who dumped me. If she wants me back, she needs to get on her fucking knees and beg." She'd already done enough damage. No matter how much I wanted her, I wouldn't cave. "Period."

"I respect that. But...what if that never happens?"

The idea of never having her again was painful, agonizing. Any other woman would be shit compared to her. But since my hands were tied, I had to let her go. She'd hurt me enough as it was... I wasn't gonna let her hurt me anymore. "Then it never happens."

14

SOFIA

COMPLICATED.

He made things fucking complicated.

I wanted easy, no strings attached. I wanted someone who meant nothing to me, whom I meant nothing to. Relationships always had the same shelf life. There was always a beginning, a middle, and an end.

There was no happily ever after...at least not in my world.

By just being lovers, the sex was always good. There was always heat. And there was no commitment, no expectation. He didn't own me, so he couldn't possess me, couldn't knock me around to punish me.

I didn't belong to him.

But Hades had pushed me too far.

At first, I felt relief. The weight had been lifted from my shoulders, and I could glide. I got clean and killed my addiction. I quit cold turkey and had to keep moving. I would find another man, find someone who could please me without wanting something more.

But once a week had come and gone, the addiction started to kick in again.

I missed him.

So fucking much.

I missed the way he slid his hand into my hair and kissed me. I missed the way he gripped my ass when he said good-bye. I missed the way those brown eyes would fuck me across the room. Every kiss was heavenly, every fuck was divine.

Who was I kidding...? There was no one else like him.

Hades Lombardi was one of a kind.

I didn't want to call him and open the door to our complicated relationship. But I also wanted to get laid...and get laid good. I had to decide what I wanted—and how much I wanted it. It was becoming obvious that Hades would continue to push for more with me, to get me to open my shattered heart and hand it over to him.

Never gonna happen.

But I was weak...and horny...and miserable.

So, I called.

I was sitting on the couch in my apartment with the phone against my ear. Every time it rang, I held my breath because he could pick up at any moment. It continued to ring until it went to a robotic voice messaging system.

I hung up.

I was disappointed. I'd expected him to answer.

Maybe he was with someone else. Maybe he'd already moved on. Maybe I wasn't as special to him as I thought.

Hours passed, and he didn't call me back.

Maybe he wasn't going to. Maybe all the damage I'd caused couldn't be fixed. When I told him we shouldn't see each other anymore, he wordlessly left the room and didn't look back. There was no fight. He just gave in.

Anxious, I texted him. *Can we talk?*

Silence.

I gave up and set my phone on the couch. I'd pushed away the best sex of my life. Now he was probably with someone else. Why did he have to screw everything up? Why didn't he just leave it alone? Why couldn't we be lovers who didn't give a damn about each other?

My phone started to ring.

It was him.

My heart did a somersault into my stomach before I answered.

His deep voice was scary, full of rage and annoyance. "What do you want?"

He was so cold I wasn't sure if I should hang up. I should have been stronger and not called him in the first place. Now that I was faced with his hostility, I realized this plan was stupid. My hormones never should have been put in charge.

"I asked you a question."

My god, he was terrifying. "I'm sorry I called…"

"If you meant that, you wouldn't have called me in the first place. Say what you have to say."

I didn't realize how gentle he'd been with me in the past now that I was facing this different version of him. This must be the drug-dealer version, the villain I never met. "I miss you…that was all I had to say."

His response was silence.

Now I felt stupid for saying that out loud.

"What do you want me to do about that?"

Geez, he could be a dick when he was pissed. "Nothing. I just—"

"Bullshit. It's ten o'clock right now. You want me to come over there and fuck you. That's what you want me to do about it."

I couldn't believe this was the same man who'd placed my hand over his heart and vowed he would never hurt me. He was sensitive, passionate…kind. "Yes…"

"And why would I want to do that?"

As if he'd punched me in the stomach, I felt my lungs deflate. I felt embarrassed, assuming he would want what I wanted.

"You dumped me, remember? You think I'm just gonna come crawling back like some kind of pussy?"

Definitely not.

"No, Sofia. Fuck you." Click.

He hung up on me.

I lowered the phone to my side, ripped apart by that cold insult. He made me feel weak. He humiliated me. He made me feel stupid for dumping him in the first place. He made me feel even dumber for calling him. And he made me want him even more...because I couldn't have him.

I picked up the phone and called him again.

He answered immediately. "Yes?"

"I'm sorry, okay?"

Silence.

"I'm sorry I reacted that way. You were just...suffocating me. I told you a million times I don't want anything serious, but you kept pressuring me. I'm not going to change my mind, so just let it go."

Silence.

"I'd like to be with you...but under those conditions."

"Your conditions?" he asked coldly.

"Yes..."

"Well, here are mine." His voice lowered in volume but turned more sinister. "Get on your fucking knees and apologize to me. Your conditions can fuck off."

A FEW DAYS passed as I tried to shrug off my last conversation with Hades. The smart thing to do was forget about him since our relationship was so tense now. But after a couple days, I started to miss him again.

And actually consider his request.

I was working at the hotel, daydreaming about the man I couldn't have. I missed the connection between our souls, the way our hearts beat as one. I missed the taste of his sweat on my tongue, the way my nails sank into his skin. All I had to do was put on a short dress and pick up a guy at the bar, but I didn't want to do that.

There was only one man I wanted.

I grabbed my phone and texted him. *I get off in twenty minutes...*

I never got a response back.

Ten minutes later, Hades walked inside, dressed in a black jacket and dark jeans. Boots were on his feet, and a gray scarf was around his neck. He walked through the lobby and ignored me, heading straight to his regular room.

I was scared of him over the phone. Imagined how scared I would be when I faced him in person.

When my shift was over, I made my way to room 402.

My heart was pumping almost in my throat, full of adrenaline and fear. I could turn back and abandon ship, but I wanted him too much to do the smart thing. I wanted to do the reckless thing.

I walked through the door then came face-to-face with him. Tall and muscular, he stood in front of me, his scarf and jacket hung on the back of the chair at the dining table. That erotic gaze he used to give me was long gone, replaced by an expression of such fury that he looked like a hit man.

I never let anyone steal my confidence or make me uncomfortable, but he made me want to shake everywhere.

"You have something to say to me?" His deep voice was low but full of command like the ruler of the world. His jaw was covered in a sexy shadow, his hair was styled the way I liked. His body was pumping with blood, so his muscles looked thicker than usual. He also looked angrier than usual.

I couldn't believe I was about to succumb to his commands. I thought I had more strength than that. Had more self-respect than that. But I wanted this night to end one way—with us in bed together.

So, I swallowed my pride and lowered myself to my knees.

He watched me, his jaw tightening as he watched me kneel on the carpet and pull my dress to my thighs. He stepped closer to me, looming over me like a general about to bark orders.

"I'm sorry…"

"Didn't hear you."

I cleared my throat, suffocating in self-loathing. "I'm sorry."

"For what?"

"I'm sorry for…getting upset."

"Try again." He crossed his arms over his chest.

"I'm sorry for ending things."

"Wrong again."

I sighed. "I'm sorry for hurting you..." I lowered my gaze because the humiliation was too much.

"Look at me when you talk to me."

I lifted my gaze.

"Repeat what you just said."

"I'm sorry for hurting you."

"Anything else you want to add? Because I'm not sure if I've forgiven you."

This man was a hard-ass. "I miss you...a lot. I haven't been with anyone else because you're all I want. I already told you I don't want anything serious. When I said that, I meant it. But I do want you...and it's hard to live without you."

He stared at me for a long time, considering my apology like a judge issuing a ruling. He pulled his shirt off and set it on the chair, revealing his chiseled physique and the happy trail that led into his jeans.

I knew I'd been forgiven.

"Get your ass up." He gave me his hand and helped me up.

My hands went to his chest so I could finally feel him, finally kiss him.

He grabbed me by the elbow and positioned me back, forcing me to look at him head on. "I only forgive people once—not twice. Fuck with me again, and it's over. When you call, I won't answer. When you need me, I won't be there. Do you understand me?" His fingers dug into my arm.

Hades had never shown me this side of him before, and I wasn't sure if I liked it. It was unnerving on the one hand, but also sexy on the other. This must be the way he treated his enemies, even his allies. "I understand."

He released my arm then placed his hand on my shoulder. He gave a subtle push, lowering me back down to my knees. When I was on the carpet, he reached for his belt and loosened it before he pulled down his zipper. His rock-hard cock appeared a moment later, thick like a steel rod. "Show me how much you missed me."

Now I was back where I started—on my back with Hades between my legs. I'd stayed clean for a week, but barely. I caved quickly, needing his essence in my veins, needing his come deep inside me. My nails clawed down his back as our faces came together, the muscles of his strong back working to thrust inside me just the way I liked.

I kept coming...over and over. My feet hurt from all the cramps; the pads of my fingers were soaked in his sweat. As if the last week had never happened, we fell right back into place, the heat burning us from the inside out.

God, I'd missed this.

His lips moved to my ear, and he breathed hard, his quiet moans now loud like they were projected through a speaker. "How much come can this pussy hold?"

I loved it when he talked dirty to me. He had the deepest voice, the sexiest grunts. He turned me on with just his masculine tone, especially after the way he'd ordered me around. This man was a hard-ass. I'd never wanted to be bossed around, but with him, it didn't seem so bad. "All of it."

He moaned and kept thrusting, his hand buried deep into my hair.

I grabbed his neck and positioned his mouth against mine, needing a hot kiss to hit my climax. I loved his embraces, the way he kissed me in such a manly way. Sometimes, he was gentle with me, and at other times, he kissed me like he was trying to break my lips. My fingers dug into his ass, and I pulled him into me at the perfect pace, taking him deep so I could come all over him.

I bit my lip as I hit the peak, my head rolling back as I whimpered and moaned. Tears sprang from my eyes once more, leaking down the sides of my face to the pillow underneath me. It was just so good; I couldn't keep everything bottled up inside. This bed was soaked with our tears, sweat, and come.

Hades watched me, his face tinting red as his eyes darkened. Every time he watched me come, he wasn't far behind with his own climax. He thrust then shoved himself balls deep, exploding inside my pussy for the hundredth time.

We finished together, our foreheads pressed skin-to-skin.

We both fell down slowly, like feathers gliding back down to earth. Our bodies were wrapped up in our mutual come, so sticky and warm. His cock slowly softened inside, but it still had enough definition to make me feel full.

My fingers slid into his hair, and I kissed him, feeling so satisfied after the lonely week I'd had. This was exactly what I wanted, only bliss, nothing else. I didn't want the emotional heartache from a relationship, the unavoidable staleness it eventually brought. I just wanted this...heat, passion, and lust.

He slowly pulled out of me, and like the plug in a bathtub, once his cock was gone, everything spilled out of me. He watched it with hungry eyes, proud of the contents that he'd stuffed inside me. He lay beside me, his body gleaming with sweat.

I could feel him drip out of me, feel how stuffed I was with load after load. It'd been a week since I'd last felt this way, since I'd felt like a satisfied woman. The high was so powerful that it washed away the regret I'd felt for coming back to him in the first place.

I glanced at the time on the clock. Geez, it was late. Where did the time go?

After a short rest, he got out of bed and slipped his watch back onto his wrist. Then he got to his feet and started to cover that perfect body with clothes. Normally, he wanted to stay in bed as long as possible, but now he'd had a change of heart.

"You're leaving?" I sat up in bed, still feeling the heaviness between my legs.

"Yes." He looked out the window as he pulled on his jacket, his back turned to me.

"You're still mad at me?"

"You tell me." He turned around and faced me, his eyes no longer lustful like they had been before.

I held the sheet over my chest even though he'd seen me so many times. "I thought we were okay…"

"I hold grudges—and I hold them for a long time."

"Well, I don't know what you want me to do…"

He approached the bed then sat beside me. Without warning, his hand reached for my neck and he grabbed me, made me feel like property he possessed. The deed was in his pocket, and he owned me for all time. "You're coming to my place for the weekend. Pack a bag and get comfortable."

"I have to work on Saturday."

"Then go to work and come back."

"You're mad at me, so you want me to sleep over?" I asked incredulously.

"No. I'm mad at you, so you'd better make it up to me." He pulled me in close and kissed me, giving me a hard embrace that would leave my lips swollen for the next few hours. When he pulled away, he opened his wallet and tossed tons of bills onto the bed. "Your bag better be full of lingerie."

15

HADES

I'D JUST RISEN FROM MY DESK TO LEAVE THE OFFICE WHEN Damien walked inside.

"The new cook is good."

"I know—I picked him out." I left my laptop and documents behind, intending to take care of it after the weekend. The bank I'd founded wasn't competitive in the market. There were a lot of other places that offered better returns. But mine had special services those other banks couldn't provide. The government would have to be stupid not to notice the red flags, but since my establishment held money for a lot of high-profile criminals, it was smart to look the other way.

It was a war they couldn't win.

"You want to hit a strip club tonight? Or better yet, a brothel? Throw some cash around and make two women roll around together." A dreamy look came into his eyes. "Man, I love being rich."

I adjusted my watch under my cuff link and rounded the desk. "I have plans this weekend."

"Good." He crossed his arms over his chest. "You found someone else."

"No." I leaned against the desk and faced him. "Same woman."

The corner of his mouth rose in a smile. "She came back?"

"On her knees," I said with a nod.

"Good for you. Make her work for it?"

"She still is." She was the one who'd had all the power when this relationship began, but she'd fucked that up when she left me. Now, I was in control—and I wasn't going to let go. Once she laid her cards on the table, I beat her hand and would never let her forget it.

"Ooh...that sounds hot."

"She's coming over this weekend."

"Good. Now you're headed in the right direction."

I shrugged. "She still wants the same thing. But now that she can't walk away from me, I'll just change her mind."

"Not a bad plan. You can pull it off." Damien would normally tease me for being so hung up on a woman, but since he knew this was real, he was only supportive. He was all jokes most of the time, but when I was serious, he was serious. "I don't know how to make a woman fall in love with you, but I'm sure you'll figure it out."

Damien was with me that day the gypsy read my future, but he didn't hear a single word of her message. He'd been outside the tent, and when he asked me what happened, I'd never answered. I'd been thinking about that night often, paranoid that the superstitious bullshit could actually be true. "Remember when we went to Morocco eight years ago?"

"For your twenty-first?" he asked, his eyebrow raised. "Absolutely. I got my best blow job there—and it was dirt cheap."

"Remember that gypsy we saw?"

"In the purple tent that smelled like a skunk's ass? Definitely. Why?"

"You remember your fortune?"

"Uh...I think so." He squinted his eyebrows as he tried to remember. "Something about me being rich...which did come true. And then some bullshit about a woman loving me for me...but then I leave her? I can't remember it word for word. Why do you ask?"

"Has that happened to you?" I was a grown-ass man who had made my own path in life. I wasn't successful and respected because of destiny. I made this shit happen—it didn't happen *to* me. So I refused to believe that some supernatural force in the world was actually punishing me for all the crimes I committed to get here. That I wouldn't have the woman I loved because the universe wouldn't allow it to happen. But then Sofia came into the picture...and made me question everything.

"Well, you know I'm rich."

"What about the other thing? About the girl."

"No," he said with a laugh. "Come on, that's all bullshit. You don't actually believe that, right?"

Maybe it just hadn't happened yet.

"Hades?" he pressed. "What's this about?"

"I'm just curious, that's all."

"What was your fortune?"

I lowered my gaze to the floor. "It doesn't matter. You're right. It's all bullshit."

"Hades." He stepped closer to me, cocking his head to the side so he could see my face. "I've never seen you like this before. I've never seen you scared of anything. But now you're scared of something, and I don't even know what it is. I'm your best friend...so tell me." He grabbed my shoulder and gave me a squeeze. "Come on."

My hands gripped the edge of my desk as I lifted my chin once more. I didn't make eye contact, choosing to stare at the closed door to my office. "She told me that I would be punished for everything I'd done."

"Be punished how?"

I sighed before I answered, letting all the air out of my lungs. "That I would only love one woman...and she would never love me back."

Damien didn't laugh even though anyone else would have. My words sounded ridiculous as I said them. He must have thought the same thing. But he respected me too much to make me feel stupid for saying that out loud. "And you think Sofia is the only woman you'll ever love?"

My eyes shifted back to the ground. "Yeah...that's what I'm afraid of."

————————

HELENA LET SOFIA INSIDE, and I met her in the entryway.

A black bag was over her shoulder, and she examined the art pieces on my wall, the sculpture in the center of the room that had a vase of flowers on top. Her hand gripped the strap of her bag, and she visibly looked uncomfortable standing there, like she was being marched to prison for a crime she didn't commit.

I'd spent the afternoon convincing myself that my future wasn't already written, that this was just a coincidence. I didn't love her. I was just obsessed with the chase, fascinated by this woman's indifference. Everything else in life was so easy to attain...except her. That's all it was, nothing more.

But as I watched her standing there, the same feelings swept over me. My lips ached to kiss her curved bottom lip, to suck in her breath until it filled my lungs. My fingers ached to feel those strands of hair, to fist them so hard that she couldn't move away. My dick ached to be inside her. The rhythm of my heart suddenly changed, going from a slow and steady beat to a rapid sprint. My neck suddenly felt warm from a rise in temperature, and every part of my body suddenly felt sensitive, as if I could feel her energy as it pulsed in the room.

Maybe it wasn't about the chase.

I halted in front of her and didn't kiss her like I usually did. I noticed the way she took a deep breath and slightly parted her lips, like she expected a smooch right off the bat. My fingers moved to her shoulder and lifted the strap from her body. "Did you get what I asked?"

She gave a nod.

I took her hand and guided her up the stairs.

The top floor was my private area, where I had my gym, my office, and my bedroom. The other two floors were Helena's domain, where she cleaned and kept the place tidy for potential guests. The only time she ventured into my quarters during the day was while I was at work.

And I'd told her I wanted my privacy this weekend.

Sofia had seen my home before, but she'd never spent any extended time there. She walked beside me and examined the beige curtains, the artwork that lined the walls. She peered into the open doorway that led to my office but didn't ask any questions.

Then we entered my bedroom, the largest room in the house. I had a huge balcony that overlooked the city, a bathroom with a tub big enough to fit several adults, and a walk-in shower with two showerheads. The whole place was more than enough for several people, not just two lovers.

I set her bag on the end of the bed. "Change."

"What's wrong with what I'm wearing?"

I turned to her, annoyed with her dark jeans and sweater. "Is that lingerie?"

"No..."

"Then change."

She took her bag into the bathroom and shut the door behind her.

I stripped down to my boxers then lay on the bed, my head propped up on a pillow. My hand rested on my chest as my dick got hard in my shorts. Just imagining how she would look made me want to blow, to come in my shorts like a teenage boy.

She came out a moment later, wearing a one-piece bodysuit that was so lacy I could see her skin underneath. It was virgin-white, and she had matching garters up her slender thighs. She'd volumized her hair and added a bit of mascara to make her eyes pop. It had a crotch that unfastened, so I could fuck her without taking it off.

Good.

I propped myself up and stared at her, my expectations met. I preferred black, but the white looked so sexy on her dark skin. She had the perfect body to pull off something so slimming. The deep plunge in the front showed off her perky tits, and her legs looked so sexy in those lacy garters.

Damn.

I pushed my boxers down so she could see my stamp of approval. "Get over here."

She crawled onto the bed then moved toward me, on all fours.

My hand slid into her hair, and I pulled her in for a kiss. Her body slowly molded into mine as I ran my hand up her thigh, feeling the lace under my fingertips. My lips kissed her neck, her chest, and the shell of her ear. Then I kissed her again. She was so fucking sexy, but I wasn't in a hurry to fuck her.

Just wanted to kiss her.

"YOU REALLY WANT me to dress like this while we have dinner?" She wore a black teddy with garters.

"Yes."

"I'm practically naked."

"That's the point." I sat across from her and poured two glasses of wine.

Her tits were pressed together, and the lacy fabric wouldn't protect her if something hot fell into her lap. But she looked sexy in lingerie, and I liked having all the power.

Especially since she gave it to me.

I cut into my steak and ate, pairing it with the red wine Helena had picked out. My phone kept vibrating and buzzing because work never stopped, so I put it on silent to keep it from ruining our dinner.

"You don't have to turn it off because of me." Her hair was done in big curls, and she wore enough makeup to look like a stripper. But I liked her that way, as a woman who willingly became my prisoner.

"You're much more interesting."

"I find that hard to believe..." It was one of the rare times we'd shared a meal together, and it was clear she didn't eat much. Whenever food was in front of her, she took a few bites of then lost interest. It was probably why she had such a nice figure—because she didn't care about food.

Wine, on the other hand…was a different story.

She looked out the large windows to the patio, probably enjoying the view just the way I did. Normally, I'd sit outside, but now that December was almost upon us, it was far too cold. But we still got to enjoy the view. "How long have you lived here?"

"You can ask me anything, and that's what you decide on?" I'd noticed she picked questions that would never have substantial answers. Even now, she was keeping everything sterile, doing her best to make us strangers.

"I'm genuinely curious. This place looks like it was remodeled recently."

"I moved in eight years ago."

"You like living in the city?"

"Prefer it. Tuscany is too vulnerable."

"It's beautiful…"

"Yes, but you become an easy target."

"So, you feel safer in the city?"

"It's a lot easier to keep eyes stationed everywhere—out of sight."

"So, you have men watching your property at all times?"

I nodded. "If an enemy comes too close…" I squeezed my forefinger like it was on top of a trigger.

"Well...good thing they knew I was friendly." She drank her wine again, preferring the drink over her meal.

"Beautiful women are always welcome in my house."

"We can be evil too."

"That makes them even better." I took another bite of the steak, enjoying the tenderness. Helena had been working for me for a long time, and I would employ her until she was physically unable to keep up with me.

"So...you aren't working all weekend?"

"Damien has it covered."

"How did you get guys meet?"

"University."

"Really?" she asked, visibly surprised by the revelation.

"Yes, I'm smart enough to attend college."

"That's not what I meant," she said quickly. "The two of you just don't seem average... That's all."

"We were in school for one year when we decided to drop out. The classes were a joke, and there was nothing we were interested in besides becoming rich. There seemed to be quicker ways of doing that, better ways."

"So that's all you care about? Making money."

I didn't want to be stripped down to a superficial person, but maybe I was a superficial person. "Yes, it's important to me. And anyone who tells you it's not is a liar—including you."

"Me?" she asked in surprise. "No...you're mistaken."

"I'm right on the money," I said coldly. "You don't want to be married because you want to retain your independence. You want to own your hotels so you can control them. You want to be completely self-sufficient so you never have to need anyone's help. That's exactly the same thing. Financial security is freedom. So, don't make assumptions about me unless you're prepared to make them about yourself."

When she didn't have a rebuttal, she must have internalized what I said. "I'm not obsessed with being rich, but I guess the rest of that is true."

She was ambitious like me. She wanted control over everything, so she would never have to answer to anyone. If I got to control her every day of my life, I'd be a happy man. But she wanted the exact same thing...to live without tyranny.

I would be a fucking tyrant.

"There's nothing wrong with feeling that way," I said. "The better you understand who you are, the more you'll understand what you want." I continued to eat my dinner even though she was already finished.

"You and Damien seem close."

"We are."

"Is he your brother?"

"No."

"Just your friend?"

I nodded. "My only friend."

"I'm not your friend?" she whispered.

The last thing I wanted to be considered was a friend. I'd

take lover, but I preferred something better. "No. Friends don't fuck the way we do." I refilled my glass with wine and took another drink.

"I should have asked this sooner, but when we were apart... were you with anyone else?"

I wanted to blurt out the truth, but that would be stupid. It would make me seem weak, like I was sitting home alone wondering what to do about her. "That's none of your business. The second you left this relationship—"

"It's not a relationship."

I set down my glass and leaned forward. "It is a relationship. When you get on your knees and apologize, that's a fucking relationship. It's you and me...figuring this shit out." I sat back again after my tone sank into her flesh. "I'm clean. That's all you need to know."

"By your logic, you should tell me if you did or didn't. Because that's a relationship."

"Good. So you finally agree that's what this is."

"Never said those words. But according to what you just said, telling me the truth would be the right thing to do."

I hated that she was smart. But if she weren't, I probably wouldn't be so infatuated with her. "Why do you want to know so badly?"

"For my own health. Isn't that reason enough?"

"Or you're jealous." My eyes burned into hers, wanting her to admit that fact. It would be a pleasure to think about, to know she was home alone missing me, worried I was fucking some other enthused woman.

"I'm not jealous. I just know you like prostitutes, so..." She rested her fingertips on her glass, displaying the best poker face I'd ever seen. It was possible she was telling the truth, that her curiosity didn't stem from possessiveness.

"I told you I'm clean. What does it matter? The only reason it would is because you're jealous."

She dragged her fingertip across the surface of her glass.

"If you really want to know, admit the truth. But if you aren't...then my results should be good enough."

Her finger kept dragging in circles, and she watched her movements. She was quiet a long time, bringing the conversation to an end.

I hid my disappointment. When we were together, it seemed like there was something more there on her part, that she needed me more than she realized. I swore I could see it, swore I could feel it. But maybe I was wrong. Maybe this woman really didn't give a damn about me...and never would.

"Fine..." She pulled her fingertips from her glass and looked at me, her green eyes gorgeous when they reflected the candlelight. "I want to know...so I guess that means I'm jealous."

I stopped my smile from showing and felt a rush of hope in my chest. That fortune really was bullshit. It was just a stupid story the gypsy made up for a couple of coins. I was seeing something that wasn't there, losing sight of reality and focusing on stupidity. Sofia was mine. It would just take her some time to get there. "I've only been with you."

16

SOFIA

Esme sat across from me in the booth, looking like she'd just taken a shower and done her makeup even though she'd put in a full shift before meeting me for a drink. She was living her best life, enjoying being single until she finally felt like settling down. She made enough money to have her own apartment, so she didn't need to find a husband until she actually fell in love.

I'd thought growing up in a wealthy family would ensure I never had to marry unless I absolutely wanted to, but that wasn't the case.

"So, you're still seeing that hot guy?" Esme stirred her martini as she waited for an answer.

"I'm not really seeing him..."

"But you're sleeping with him, right?"

"Technically."

"And only sleeping with him?"

"Uh...technically."

She chuckled. "You're sticking to your guns, huh?"

"I'm not sticking to anything. That's just the honest truth."

"For years, you've been saying you never want to get married. I guess you really meant that, because you're screwing the perfect man, but you still haven't changed your mind."

"Yes, he's beautiful, but he's not perfect."

"What's wrong with him?"

I told her about all the stuff going on with the hotel, and of course, she was shocked. She didn't expect it; no one did. "And he owns a bank that launders a lot of cash. I guess he's also a drug dealer too."

"No way. He doesn't look like he would be one."

I shrugged. "I'm starting to realize the world isn't a warm and bubbly place."

"Guess not. So, if he weren't a drug dealer, you'd be interested?"

"Not necessarily. After watching my mother's first and second marriages, I'm just not interested. Breakups are always really nasty affairs. And relationships that last are usually worse in the long run. I understand a couple staying together to have children, but other than that, they just don't make sense."

"Yeah, I guess I see what you mean." She kept stirring her drink.

"I just want to run our hotel and live my life. I don't want to be pressured into getting married. Not all men get married, so why do women have to get married?"

She shrugged. "Kids?"

"I guess. But Hades keeps trying to push me into a commitment."

"Honestly, that's kind of romantic." She took a drink. "This guy wants you all to himself and doesn't want to share."

"I suppose..."

A couple of guys joined us, tag-teaming us with free drinks. One of the guys immediately went to Esme and started the conversation with a joke, which must have been funny because she laughed. They hit it off pretty quickly and kept to themselves in the corner of the booth.

My guy was cute, and since he was nice, I didn't want to waste his time. "I'm seeing someone."

"I usually assume that every time I meet a beautiful woman. It's just the odds, you know? But since my friend is—" he glanced at them and chuckled "—already making out with your friend, I guess we could keep talking."

"Yeah, I don't see the harm in that."

———

"LET ME WALK YOU HOME." Lance walked beside me, wearing his thick coat to fight the cold.

"I just live a few blocks from here. I'll be fine."

"Really? Because my apartment is in the same direction. So I can walk behind you like a weirdo, or we can walk together."

"Wouldn't want you to look like a weirdo," I said with a laugh.

We headed down the street together then approached my building.

I said goodnight on the sidewalk. "Well, it was nice to meet you." I gave a wave before I turned away.

Instead of leaving me alone, he moved into my body and kissed me.

"Whoa…" I pushed against his chest. "You need to back up, man." My purse hung across my chest, and thankfully it was right in between us, pressed into my body, so it gave me a few inches of space. "I think you had too much to drink."

"No. You're just really pretty, and I had to go for it."

"Well, I have a boyfriend." The situation was getting tenser by the second. He'd seemed like a nice guy at the bar. Talking to him didn't feel like an invitation to sex. But now, it seemed like he wanted to get his way—no matter the cost.

"He doesn't need to know anything." He moved into me again.

Instinct kicked in, and I punched him in the face. "Don't touch me." I only had seconds to figure out what to do. If I opened my purse and dug for my phone, I would be vulnerable to an attack. If I ran up the stairs to my apartment, I probably wouldn't make it there in time. I had to fish out my keys too.

He turned with the hit then grabbed his nose. "Wow…that was unnecessary." When he turned back to me, he wiped his nose, and a couple drops of blood were on his fingertip.

"Just leave me alone, alright? Go home." I was rigid on the spot, unsure what to do. It was late at night, and no one was around. I could scream, but who would hear me? Who would call the police? How long would it take them to get there?

"You should at least let me inside to clean up."

Yeah fucking right. "Go."

He stood still.

"What are you doing?"

"Waiting for you to go to your door. I'm still a gentleman."

I saw right through that bullshit. Once I got the door unlocked, he would push me inside and gag me. He wanted to hold me down and get what he wanted out of me—even if that meant he had to rape me.

How did this happen?

How the hell did I get myself in this situation?

I turned around and headed back where I came from. If I returned to the main road where the bar was, there were bound to be other people there. I could get a ride to Hades's place and stay there for the night.

"Where do you think you're going?" He grabbed me by the elbow and started to drag me into the alley.

"Get off!" I kicked him hard in the shin then threw my elbow into his face. He was a big guy, but I used enough force to make him falter. "Help!" I started to run again.

He tripped me so I fell to the ground, hidden from the road

because we were in between two buildings. His hand covered my mouth, and he yanked up my dress.

I tried to buck him off and bite him, but I couldn't. This man was twice my weight. I couldn't get my body free even if it meant the difference between life and death. I tried to roll away, but it was no use. I pushed my jaw out and finally got some of his skin. I bit down hard, but there was hardly anything to bite into.

"Bitch." He grabbed a plastic bag that had been dropped on the ground.

"No!"

He shoved it over my head and suffocated me.

I struggled to breathe, but every time I sucked in air, I just got the bag. Now my attention was focused on surviving, so he would have no problem getting my dress up and my panties down.

Was this how I was going to die?

This was it? My last moments on earth?

His heavy body was suddenly thrown off mine. Lance groaned when he was kicked by someone. Footsteps were audible in the alleyway. Someone must have heard my struggle and come to save me.

I got the bag off my head and finally breathed. My hands went to my neck, and I sucked air into my lungs, gasping because I was about to pass out from lack of oxygen. I could hear the sound of fists smashing against bone, could hear the moment Lance's body became lifeless. But the hits continued.

I picked myself up off the ground and gasped when I saw who'd saved me.

Hades was still punching him, his knuckles bloody. He held on to the front of his shirt and smashed his face in. It was so bloody, his features were no longer distinguishable. Minutes ago, he was a handsome man. Now he was just a bloody corpse.

"Stop. You'll kill him."

"He is dead." He gave him one more hard punch before he let Lance's head hit the concrete. As if nothing had happened, he got to his feet and wiped his bloody hands on his jeans. When he moved to me, his rage was gone, replaced by gentle concern. "Baby, are you alright?" He kneeled in front of me, examining my features for signs of injury.

My dress was down now and my panties were on, so he didn't have to see me like that. I survived the fight without a scratch. The only scar I had was the memory of almost being raped in an alleyway. I blurted the first question that came to mind. "How did you know...?" Was he watching me? Having his men tail me?

He nodded to my purse. "You accidentally called me. I listened for a few seconds and knew something was wrong. I drove over here right away and saw him drag you into the alleyway." Now that Lance was dead, his violence disappeared too. He seemed relieved I was okay, grateful nothing had happened to me, grateful that my phone was jostled in the fight and called him. "How many times have I told you not to walk home alone?"

I was too embarrassed to answer.

"Are you going to listen to me now?"

I nodded.

"You think you're invincible, but you aren't."

"You think I don't know that now?" I whispered. "What do we do with him?"

"Don't worry about it."

"But the police..."

"The police won't do anything. It'll be considered a missing persons case."

"How...?"

He helped me to my feet. "Because they do whatever I tell them to do."

———

HE SCRUBBED his knuckles in the bathroom sink for what seemed like an hour before all the blood and bits of flesh came off. It didn't seem to disturb him in the least, that he'd just killed someone he didn't even know. It wasn't only a murder, but murder from being beaten to death.

I took a shower when we got to his place because I felt dirty after being pinned to the alley. I also wanted to wash off Lance's touch, get rid of any trace of DNA found on my body. I dried my hair with a towel then got into his bed.

Hades joined me minutes later.

"Thanks for letting me stay here."

He cuddled me into his side and wrapped his powerful arms

around me, reminding me that no one could bother me while I was his. "You're welcome here anytime." His lips rested against the back of my neck, and he kissed me. His mouth migrated to my shoulder and then to my ear, layering me with affection.

"Do you feel weird?" I whispered.

"How?"

"That you just killed someone..."

His hand rubbed across my belly. "I kill people all the time, baby."

"But not innocent people."

His voice suddenly turned cold. "He wasn't innocent. If I'd let him live, he would have come back to your apartment. And if he didn't, he would have done that to some other girl. He probably already has. He's not innocent—and he deserved to die like that. Don't waste your time thinking about him a second longer. He's gone—end of story."

Death was irreversible, so this was permanent. That man was never coming back. It seemed like such a harsh price to pay for what he did, but I never would have felt safe if he had lived. He probably would have killed me anyway, suffocated me with that bag and then kept raping me until he was finished.

Hades was right—I shouldn't mourn his death.

I was glad he was dead.

WHEN I WOKE up the next morning, Hades had just gotten out of the shower. With a towel wrapped around his waist, he picked out his outfit for the day from his closet. A black tie with a navy-blue suit and a cream-colored collared shirt. He also had a drawer filled with various expensive watches.

It was hard to watch him go, but I didn't expect him to stay with me all day. "That's a lot of watches."

He left his closet and came to the bed, the towel still snug around his waist. There were still a few water drops on his shoulder, and his hair was still damp even though he'd dried it with a towel. "I'm a collector."

"Didn't know that." I reached for his towel and gave it a playful tug. "When did you become shy?"

He grinned before he tugged it loose and let it fall to the floor.

I stared at his nice dick and reached out my fingers to stroke his balls.

He tensed slightly when I touched him, and within seconds, his dick increased to an impressive size. He was hard and ready to fuck.

I kicked the sheets back so he could join me. I went to sleep in the nude last night because I hadn't had any clothes besides the ones on my back. It gave him easy access—if he wanted it.

"So, I'm your boyfriend?" His knees sank into the mattress as he moved on top of me.

I had no idea what provoked the question. I spread my knees and pulled him close to me. "I never said that."

"Really? I heard you say it last night."

When I'd tried to get that asshole to go away, I'd blurted out those words. I wasn't thinking at the time, just saying whatever was necessary to get him to leave me alone. There had been no merit in it, but I didn't want to ruin this moment with cruel honesty. "Don't remember."

"I do." He pinned my knees back as he brought our bodies close together. "Are you sure you want to do this?"

I wouldn't give last night another moment of my time. I'd learned my lesson, and now I would never walk home again. If Hades hadn't been there to save me, my life would have taken a dark turn...or ended altogether. But that didn't happen. "God, yes." I grabbed his ass and pulled him deep inside me, feeling my toes curl when he was all the way in. "Yes."

17

HADES

I EXAMINED THE KILOS OF METH THAT WERE READY TO BE shipped and looked at the inventory sheet. Slightly over four hundred kilos of crystal were ready to be delivered to Milan, one of my most profitable cities in the country. There were smaller dealers who infringed on my territory, assholes with a tiny lab set up in their bedrooms, but since their product was so inferior and cheap, I didn't give them the time of day.

The wolf doesn't concern himself with the sheep, right?

I signed off on the paperwork so it could be shipped hundreds of miles north, disguised as cargo for a cheese company. I made appearances at every station in my lab, popping up randomly so my men would never know when I might catch them with their pants down. Damien did the same thing—so everyone walked on eggshells.

Damien took the clipboard and glanced over it. "What did you do with the body?" He did his own check.

"Oil drum."

"And where is that?"

"Buried somewhere in the middle of Tuscany." The guy hadn't been a criminal who competed with my ranks, but he wasn't an innocent person who should have walked free. He'd tried to rape my woman—even kill her. I enjoyed beating him to death. My knuckles were still sore, but that pain only reminded me how much I had caused him to feel.

"Is she alright?"

"Yeah. She bounced back pretty quickly."

"That's good. I bet she learned her lesson…"

She'd slowly floated back down to earth after the traumatic event took place. Then she brushed it off and kept going, almost like it never happened at all. She still wanted to sleep with me as if some man hadn't just tried to force himself on her. It made me respect her, how tough she was. "Yeah. She won't be walking home alone anytime soon."

"I'm surprised you're taking this so well." He handed the clipboard off to one of the guys then walked with me to the counter.

"I killed the guy, didn't I?" With my bare hands.

"But what if she hadn't butt-dialed you?" His phone started to ring, but he silenced it and set it on the counter.

I didn't want to think about that. "That didn't happen, so it doesn't matter." If I had it my way, she'd be living with me, escorted everywhere she went by my best guys. All men would be afraid to look at her longer than a nanosecond. But that lack of independence was exactly what she didn't want. She refused to let one bad night make her afraid to live.

Damien let it go. "Need anything?"

"I'm not the one who was assaulted."

"Yeah, but it probably hurt you a million times more than it hurt her."

WHEN SHE STEPPED out of the hotel, I was waiting for her.

She wore a black pea coat with gold buttons along with tights and black boots. Her brown hair was straight and still perfectly styled despite working five hours at the lobby counter. With her hands in her pockets for warmth, she walked to the edge of the sidewalk and prepared to wave down a cab.

Good girl.

She didn't see me standing to the left, and she didn't notice my black car parked along the curb. She was probably eager to go home and get out of the cold. She pulled her phone out of her pocket and started to text.

I came up behind her but stopped when my phone vibrated in my pocket. I pulled it out and looked at the screen. *I'm about to get in a cab. Should I give the driver my address or yours?*

"Mine."

At the sound of my voice, she turned around, both surprised and happy to see me. It was late at night, but we were still in public. That didn't stop her from moving into my chest and wrapping her arms around my neck. She seemed to forget about the cameras everywhere, the fact that a coworker could see her at any second.

Or maybe she just didn't care anymore. I chose to believe that. "Want to get a drink?"

"Sure." She leaned in the rest of the way and kissed me.

My arms tightened around her waist and pulled her close to me, keeping her warm by chasing away the cold. I breathed fire into her cold lips, made her tits relax under her coat. I guided her to my car next and seated her in the passenger seat.

The assault had been part of a terrible night that I tried not to think about. But it also seemed to change our relationship. Instead of seeing me as a threat or a dictator, she saw me as a savior. I was the man who protected her, not hurt her. Now she was more relaxed around me, taking down her walls instead of putting them up.

Maybe it was exactly what we needed.

I drove to the bar and handed my keys to the valet before we walked inside. With my arm around her waist, I was immediately guided to the best booth in the place, something with privacy but also with the attention of the best server.

"What are you having?" I watched her peel off her coat and reveal her gray sweater dress underneath. It was tight on her chest and arms, showing off the curves I'd become infatuated with. I could have just driven her home and hiked up her dress, but the parameters of our relationship had changed.

"I'll have whatever you have."

"Double scotch neat?" I asked, encouraging her to get something else.

"I can handle it."

"I'd rather you not be drunk when we get home."

She rolled her eyes. "I come from a family of drinkers. I can handle it."

I gave the order, and we were left alone.

My arm was around her shoulders, and I sat close to her, close enough to kiss her if I felt like it. My fingers brushed the hair out of her face so I could get a better look at her, the piece of art that I alone got to enjoy.

Her hand moved to my thigh under the table, squeezing me through my jeans. "How was your day?" She spoke in a sexy whisper, adopting a tone a woman would use in dirty talk.

"Fine."

"Fine?" she asked. "That's not much of an answer."

"Do you really want to know?"

"Why else would I have asked?"

The waitress brought the drinks.

I picked up my glass and held it up for a toast.

She smiled then picked hers up.

"To good sex and strong liquor." I tapped my glass against hers before I took a drink.

She brought it to her lips and tried to drink like a man, getting a rush of it down her throat. She almost choked it back up, but she forced it down into her stomach. She wiped away the drops with her thumb.

I downed my entire glass and tried not to chuckle at her. "I warned you."

She stuck out her tongue and made a disgusted face. "How the hell do you drink that?"

"Lots of practice. Every day." My hand moved into her hair and rested on the back of her neck. "And if you want to prove yourself to me, do it in the bedroom. I don't give a damn how much or little you can drink."

"Good." She made a grossed-out face again. "I think I'm done for the night. For the week, actually."

I grabbed her glass and finished it off.

"Are you going to be able to drive?"

"Baby, I could fly a plane right now." I drank all the time, even held my most important meetings over a bottle of the finest scotch. It was a staple of my diet, the next best thing after water.

"So...you were going to tell me about your day."

"Damien and I prepared our next shipment to Milan. Four hundred kilos. Then I had a meeting at the bank. I'm holding on to blood money for the mafia until the dust settles for them. Then I worked out. What about you?"

She blinked a few times as she absorbed what I'd said. "You shipped out a ton of crystal then met the mafia? All in one day?"

"And it's only Tuesday."

She stared at me incredulously before she looked away. "My day was pretty boring. Slept in then worked at the hotel."

"Not going to work with Gustavo anymore?"

Her gaze drifted away, and she turned quiet. "I haven't decided what I'm going to do about that yet."

I didn't open the conversation because I knew it would only dampen her mood. "Want to go to my place or yours?"

"My apartment is a shithole compared to yours."

"But it has a bed—that's all we need."

"But you also have a cook…"

"You like Helena?" I asked, enjoying her preference for my place.

"Duh. She's amazing."

"So, you like my place for the sex and the food?"

"Yep. It's like a hotel."

I opened my wallet and set cash on the table. "Then let's go. Let me know what you want for dinner, and I'll tell Helena on the way."

"Ooh…this is going to be a great night."

———

HER FACE WAS PRESSED against the sheets, and her smeared mascara stained the off-white fabric. Her cries were muffled as the tears streaked down her cheeks to her lips. Her ass was proudly in the air, her back arched deeply, and her nails dug into my knees.

Every time my dick moved deep inside her, her asshole tightened. I stared at it as I fucked her, obsessed with every single curve she possessed. I could write a goddamn poem about that asshole because it was so perfect. At some point, I was going to fuck it as hard as I fucked her pussy.

"Hades…" She gripped my knees and bounced back against me, loving my big cock inside her. She couldn't get enough of it, addicted to it just the way I was addicted to her. Her cream built up at my base, piling up with its sexy white color.

My hands gripped her hips, and my fingers dug into her tummy, yanking her down my length as I thrust inside her. My thumbs rubbed against her cheeks, pulling them apart so I could keep staring at that sweet little asshole.

I fucked her like an animal—and she liked it.

"God…yes." We'd been this way for forty minutes, fucking like maniacs. Load after load, we kept going, her pussy dripping with my come. I fucked her like a whore but loved her like a soul mate.

I could do this for the rest of my life…easily.

The thought made me slow down for a second, made me consider the gravity of what I'd just said to myself. I'd been in this exact position before, having good sex with a beautiful woman, but I'd never felt something so profound. What made her different? What made her special?

I didn't have a single reason.

There was no reason.

I just felt the way I did...because that was how I wanted to feel.

I pressed my palm against her lower back and steadied her as I came, my cock throbbing as I sent another deposit deep inside that tight pussy. Waves of pleasure radiated through me everywhere. I shivered in ecstasy, closing my eyes as I enjoyed her. With every climax, the sensation was supposed to get weaker.

With her, it got better.

I pulled out my cock and watched my come drip from her pussy. It was an erotic sight, seeing all the damage I caused to that perfect cunt. Her asshole still stared at me, as if it was begging me to fuck her.

She relaxed on the bed and turned onto her side, tired and spent from the fucking we'd just done. Her hair was a curtain behind her, and she immediately closed her eyes.

I went into the shower to rinse off and get ready for bed. I let the warm water flow over me as I closed my eyes. A sense of peace washed over me, a calm reservoir I wanted to drink from forever. The last ten years of my life had been a tidal wave. I was constantly running from one place to the next.

But now I wanted to stay still.

When I'd pictured my future, I was either alone or dead. I didn't expect to live long in this line of business, and if I died, my legend would survive long after I was gone. There were always women in the picture, and as I aged, they stayed the same. Damien was in this vision...because I couldn't picture my life without him.

But now someone else was in the picture too.

The sound of the shower door caused my eyes to open.

Sofia joined me under the spray, tilting her head back so the water would soak into her hair. She naturally arched her back, showing off her flat belly and her slender legs.

My eyes immediately shifted down to look at her.

She closed her eyes and ran her fingers through her hair.

She stole my hot water and interrupted my zen moment, but having her there was much better than being alone. My hands grabbed her slender waist, and I pulled her close to me, getting us both under the warm flow from the showerheads.

I cupped the back of her head and kissed her, kissed her like I hadn't just fucked her for an hour straight. I pulled her close like it'd been a week since I'd last held her, since the last time we were close like this. My dick got hard like it'd been forever since I'd last gotten laid. No matter how much I had her, it was never enough. I always wanted more...always needed more. I was pussy-whipped. Obsessed. Infatuated. I was a whole different man because of this woman. I was a man I hadn't thought I was capable of being.

And I liked it.

18

SOFIA

Weeks passed, and I started to forget about the night Lance assaulted me. It felt like a bad dream, not a real-life trauma. Being with Hades gave me a sense of invincibility, like he would always protect me when I couldn't protect myself. When Esme asked me if I'd seen Lance, I pretended I had no idea what happened to him.

That was the truth. I had no idea where his body ended up. Police never came to my street, and when I passed by the alleyway, his corpse wasn't sitting there.

It was like it never happened.

For all intents and purposes, it hadn't.

I was standing at the counter when Gustavo walked up to me. He rarely spoke to me at work, doing his best to treat me like any other employee on the property. "Hello, sweetheart. How are you?"

I'd been distant with my family for a while. The truth took a long time to process, just like when the garbage disposal needed a minute to grind up all the crap I shoved into the sink. My romantic view of the world was quickly being replaced by cold reality. Everything I believed about the world was a lie. "Good. You?"

"Christmas is next week. Thinking about taking a trip to the chalet in Switzerland. Would you like to join us?"

It felt wrong not spending the holiday with them, but it also felt strange to leave Hades. Our relationship still wasn't a relationship to me, but he was the first thing that popped into my mind. Our heated nights at the hotel had stopped, and we spent most of our time at his place. Instead of leaving when the fun was over, I slept over and had coffee and breakfast after Hades already went to work. The fling had turned into something deeper overnight. I didn't even know how it happened because I'd worked so hard to avoid it. Now I was getting in deeper and deeper...and it would be harder to break it off.

Nothing had changed, in my opinion. I didn't want to get married, let alone to a drug dealer.

Come on, that was never going to work.

I finally answered him. "Yeah, sure."

His eyes lit up with joy because his affection for me was genuine. "That's lovely. Your mother will be very happy."

Yes, she would be thrilled to stick her nose in my business for an entire week.

"Just so you know, Barsetti Lingerie models will be checking in tonight. There's a fashion show taking place somewhere in the city. Conway Barsetti is paying for everything, so give them the five-star treatment."

"I give all our guests the five-star treatment."

He winked. "Good answer."

A FEW HOURS LATER, they arrived. Their plane had landed, and the cars pulled up to the lobby. One by one, they got out, looking like they were ready for the runway now. They didn't seem the least bit exhausted by the plane ride or the drive from the airport. With perfectly styled hair, sky-high heels, and diamond earrings, they were ready to impress.

I watched them pass, escorted by our general manager. When they approached the desk, we handed over their keys and took care of their luggage. Acting like queens, they swept their hair off their shoulders, expecting everything to be done for them.

It was a bit obnoxious.

An hour later, they finally cleared the lobby, and the hotel was quiet once again.

My shift ended, so I took a cab home. My dark apartment was small and cramped. The dining table was stuffed against the wall because there was nowhere else to put it. I only had one couch because my place was only eight hundred square feet. I wasn't ungrateful.

I was just used to nicer things.

I was used to Hades.

I opened a bottle of wine and drank on the couch while absent-mindedly watching TV. The only thing I wanted to do was reach for my phone and call Hades, but since my impulse was so strong, I purposely denied it.

How did I get so attached?

It was the sex...it had to be. I'd never gotten laid like that in all my life, never stayed wet that long because I was lucky to come even once. He was a manly man, not a boy. I told myself that was the reason...and I shouldn't blame myself.

My phone lit up with a text message. *Get your ass over here.*

My resolve disappeared because that was all I wanted to do. I didn't want to sit in this apartment alone with a bottle of red wine for company. I wanted a big, sweaty man on top of me. My fingers wanted to feel the coarse hair of his slight beard. My eyes wanted to look into his as he fucked me.

Why would I want to be here if I could be with him?

Come here, or I'll get you. Which is it going to be?

I hated being bossed around, but with him, it made me go weak. I liked it when he grabbed me by the hair and forced me to kiss him. When he pinned my arms above my head as he fucked me. When he told me I was his.

I liked everything...which was why I said no. *I'm gonna stay in tonight. I'll see you tomorrow.* I needed to break it up, to eliminate the intensity, to soften the seriousness between us. We were on a dangerous path, and I didn't want to see where it led.

I'm on my way.

WORDLESSLY, we drove back to his place.

Music played over the speakers, and the windows were tinted with frost because it was so cold outside. Red brake lights were absent because we were the only car on the road. He hit the gas and revved the powerful engine as he drove through the slick streets, only one hand on the wheel.

The other held mine.

His fingers curled around my hand, trapping it with warmth. His thumb gently brushed against my palm, lightly tracing the web of my handprint.

I turned my head slightly in the leather seat to look at him without him noticing.

His eyes quickly scanned the road ahead of him as he navigated the city, calmly pushing his car to unnecessary speed. His jawline was so sharp against his corded neck. The shadow of facial hair was noticeable under the glow of the blue light from his dashboard. His eyes had a special shine to them too. He was a beautiful man who could be anywhere tonight. He could be at a brothel, he could in the French Riviera fucking a model, he could be on a yacht off the coast of Greece.

But he was with me.

We parked in the underground garage then went to his bedroom on the top floor. He took off his watch and put it in the drawer where he kept all the others. It was always the first thing to come off his body, and it was the only item he actually took care of. Everything else was stripped away and left on the floor for Helena to deal with later.

Once my clothes were gone, our naked bodies fell onto the

bed together, my head hitting the pillow as his face hung above mine. When he'd arrived on my doorstep, he didn't say a word. We still hadn't spoken since that moment. The air was full of tension because of it, full of the static electricity that erupted between our bodies.

His arms moved behind my knees, and he pulled me wide open as he prepared to take me, heavy cock resting on my excited clit. He rubbed nose against mine as he looked at me, his lips brushing over mine like he teasing me.

My fingers moved into his hair, and I pulled him in for a kiss. The desire he showed me made me feel like one of the Barsetti models, like I was beautiful enough to capture this man's focus. He never made me feel less than perfect, even when my hair was wet and my makeup was gone.

He made me feel so damn sexy.

He pressed on the top of his dick and guided the tip of his shaft inside me. He pushed slowly, sinking into my tightness like it was the first time. A quiet moan came from his lips when he felt my slickness, when he glided inside until his balls hit my ass.

"Yes…" I closed my eyes and felt my lips tremble against his. My fingers pulled at his short hair, and all the nerves inside my pussy fired off in pain and pleasure. A man had never made me feel so full, had never been inside me without a condom. It was so much better skin-to-skin…especially when I got to feel his come at the end.

He rocked with forceful and even strokes, shaking me slightly as he kissed me once more. He shoved himself deep inside every time, getting his dick as far as it would go. Sometimes he tapped against my cervix, giving me a wince of pain. But knowing he was in all the way turned me on enough to forget the pain.

This was my favorite way to be together, when our mouths moved in unison and he rocked inside me. It was slow and tender sex, but he enjoyed it as much as I did. His even breathing gently escalated, his passion and exertion becoming audible.

My hand grabbed his ass and pulled him into me, my pussy gripping his length like a strong hand. He loved the curves of my body, and I loved all the muscle packed into his frame. He was a strong man, strong enough to beat a man to death.

"I'm gonna come..." My lips halted against his once I felt the tightness in my belly, the warmth that slowly spread to my extremities in preparation for a powerful event. Every phase of the orgasm was enjoyable—but the end was unbelievable. I started to writhe, holding on to him then letting go because I didn't know what else to do. My arm wrapped around his neck, and I held on to him as tears stung my eyes, as the wave swept over me and made me scream his name.

So damn good.

"Hades...Hades." My head rolled back on the pillow, and I opened my eyes, seeing him looking down at me with a stare so focused that every bone in his jaw was visible through the skin. My hands grazed up his chest as he kept rocking me, his dick so hard inside me that I bit my bottom lip harder than I meant to.

This was why I kept coming back to him. This was why I couldn't leave.

This was why I was so damn addicted.

I couldn't stop...I could never stop.

He slowed down his thrusts and pressed his forehead to mine, as if he was preparing to fill my pussy with the first load of the night. Women must have graced this bed before, but he made me feel like no one else had ever been there but me. That he'd never had sex this good with anyone else.

My hands slid up his back, and my nails clawed at his skin, waiting for that heavy warmth that would sit inside me for the rest of the night.

He closed his eyes as he focused on our bodies, as he prepared to explode inside me. His muscular arms were tight from holding his body on top of mine, from keeping my legs pinned back. His abs flexed as he thrust his hips forward, giving me his full length every single time.

I wanted to come again just watching him.

He took a deep breath, on the verge. "Marry me."

All the heat I felt seconds ago evaporated into thin air. Ice took its place, making the sheets cold on my skin, making the air too dry to breathe. It took my brain seconds to absorb what my ears had heard, and once the shock wore off, I realized I hadn't imagined it.

He just asked me to marry him.

My body went rigid underneath him. My hands halted against his chest. My heart had been racing from arousal, but now it beat rapidly for a new reason.

He pulled his head back and looked at me without shame, like he'd meant what he said and he wouldn't take it back.

He kept rocking into me like nothing happened, like we were still fucking even though all the energy was gone.

"What...?" That was all I could get out.

He moved his face back to mine and kissed me again.

The last thing I wanted was his kiss. "No." I pushed against his chest and forced him off me. I nearly tripped as I got out of bed, my foot catching on his jacket lying on the floor. Once I was steady, I didn't know what to do first. Get my clothes on and bolt for the door, or scream at him.

He'd just ruined everything.

He sat at the edge of the bed and sighed, his dick still hard and gleaming from my slickness. He stared at the floor for a second before he lifted his gaze to meet mine, sighing audibly.

"Tell me that was a joke. A really bad joke."

He got to his feet and pulled on his boxers. "It slipped out..." When he came close to me, I stepped back. Hurt entered his gaze when I steered clear of him.

"So, you didn't mean it." I didn't want to lose this man, so I was looking for any excuse to keep him. He could say it was an accident, and we could pretend it never happened. It would be awkward for a couple of weeks, but that wouldn't last forever.

His arms tensed by his sides, his gaze slowly turning cold. His jaw clenched as he mulled over his answer, savoring it on his tongue before releasing it into the air. "I wouldn't have said it unless I meant it."

No.

"I meant every word. And I'm still waiting for an answer."

Why was he doing this to me? "I already told you how I felt…"

"That was months ago. Things are different now."

"No, they aren't. I told you what I wanted. I told you I wouldn't change my mind."

His hands moved to his hips, and he kept his stare on me, his face tinting slightly with rage. The air around him started to steam. The tension was so sharp, it was cutting deep into my skin.

"You only ask someone to marry you if you love them. So, I don't understand why you asked in the first place."

His eyes narrowed slightly. "Sofia."

I didn't want to believe it. I refused to believe it. "Don't make me hurt you…"

"I'm not making you do anything."

"Yes, you are." I covered my face with my hands and slowly dragged them down, wishing this moment weren't real, that it was just a nightmare. I wasn't about to lose this man in a bitter and painful breakup.

"Sofia." He stepped closer to me then grabbed my wrists. "Look at me."

I kept my gaze averted, wanting to disassociate myself from this moment. "No…"

"Now."

My eyes shifted to his face, seeing the command in his

eyes. Hades was a man I wanted in my life, but I didn't want him close to my heart. Marriages never worked. Women became slaves. They lost their independence. They lost their ability to do anything because the man controlled every aspect of their life. They beat you or raped you. I was too young to subject myself to a relationship doomed to fail. "I don't love you..." I didn't open my heart to anyone, not even him. I was too young to give it a chance, too inexperienced to know what I wanted. How could I love a man I'd crossed off my list the moment we met?

His hands released my wrists as his eyes fell in pain. He took it as a blow to the chest, like he had been expecting me to give a different answer. His hands returned to his sides, and his pained expression slowly morphed into one of anger. "Fuck." His eyes shifted back and forth as he looked into mine before he turned away and slowly paced to the other side of the room. He ran his fingers through his hair then down his face, his fingertips resting against his lips.

I watched him absorb my response. I wished I could give him a different answer, but I'd told him what I wanted from the beginning. I told him I didn't want love or commitment. I just wanted to have fun. He kept pushing me, arrogant enough to think I would change my mind. I was only twenty-two years old... Marriage was the last thing on my mind.

I grabbed my clothes from the floor and quickly put them on.

He didn't turn around to look at me. His arms were crossed over his chest, his muscular back ripped with muscle. Everything was tight, like he was internalizing all the rage that was about to make him explode. "Get out." His voice came out quietly, a direct contradiction to the rage he was feeling.

"I told you—"

His voice rose in volume, so loud it echoed off every corner of the high ceiling. "Get the fuck out." He finally turned around and looked at me, so much hatred in his gaze. He'd loved me moments ago, but now I was the number one hit on his list. Our affection died like it had never lived in the first place. All our memories were tainted by this moment in time. Now he treated me like one of his enemies, like the man he beat to death in the alleyway. Love could turn to hate so quickly...like that was all we ever knew.

Tears welled up in my eyes and started to drip down my cheeks.

He didn't give a damn. "Goodbye, Sofia."

19

HADES

I SAT AT THE BAR WITH AN EMPTY GLASS IN FRONT OF ME. People talked around me, the TV was on in the background, and the bartender poured rounds for everyone having a good time. I couldn't even look at my watch and check the time because I was so drunk. My gaze was blurry. I had to cut myself off because I held my liquor so well that most people had no idea how intoxicated I was.

Drinking was the only solution to my problem...so that's what I did.

Sofia never called.

Not that I expected her to. Not that I wanted her to. If she did, I'd just tell her to fuck off. She made her desires very clear; she didn't want anything serious. I'd said the same sentence to so many other women. But I chose to do whatever I wanted.

It didn't stop me from hating her.

I fucking hated her.

I pulled out my phone and tried to text Damien...but I couldn't even spell. I called him instead.

He picked up immediately. "Haven't heard from you in a few days. I'm guessing you're busy with Sofia."

I didn't want to hear her name. Like someone had poured acid into my eardrums, it burned. "I need a ride."

"Why?"

"I...I just need a ride." I could barely get a single sentence out. I slurred my words and sounded idiotic.

Damien pieced the puzzle together. "Holy shit, are you drunk?"

"Just come get me." I hung up.

My phone rang again, and I struggled to take the call. "Hmm?"

"You need to tell me where you are."

"A bar." I hung up again.

He called me again. "Hang up on me again, and I'll kill you."

"I doubt it."

"What's the name of the bar?"

"Uh..." I turned to a woman sitting beside me. "Do you know where we are?"

"Santino's."

"Thanks." I winked at her and turned back to the phone. "Santino's."

She leaned forward on her stool to get my attention. "I can give you a ride home."

I was too drunk to fuck. "Nah."

"Alright," Damien said. "Sit tight. I'll be there soon."

———————

DAMIEN GOT into the driver's seat of his truck and drove me home.

I rested my head against the window, the cool temperature fighting the migraine pulsing in my temples. My eyes were closed, and I focused on the vibration of the vehicle, on the old potholes we ran over.

"Don't throw up, alright? This is a nice truck."

"Should I throw up on you, then?"

"Fuck off." He turned right then approached my building. He got through the gate and entered the underground parking garage. "So...are you going to tell me what's up? Or do I need to ask?"

I didn't want to move from my seat in the car. It wasn't comfortable, but it was better than standing. "No."

"I've never seen you drunk like this. Whatever it is, it must be bad."

"I'm fine." I pulled on the handle and opened the door...and fell on my ass.

Damien sighed. "Yeah, you look fine." He came around the truck and helped me to my feet, throwing my arm over his shoulders so he could support me to the elevator. He got me inside and then helped me take the stairs to my bedroom.

When I saw my bed, I immediately crashed on it.

I fucking hated this bed. I'd told Helena to order me a new one. I'd gotten new sheets in the meantime…so it wouldn't smell like her.

Damien pulled off my shoes.

I kicked him away. "Knock it off."

"Just shut up and hold still." He pulled off both shoes and left my socks on.

I lay on my back and stared at the ceiling, my eyes closing now that I was comfortable.

Damien pulled up an armchair close to the bed and kicked off his own shoes.

"What the fuck are you doing?"

"Making sure you don't choke on your vomit."

"I'm fine. Let me choke."

"Just shut up and go to sleep."

I was slipping away. "You shut up…"

WHEN I WOKE UP, I was sober…but I felt worse than I had last night. I dragged my hand over my face and felt the pulse in my temple. I opened my eyes and reached for my night-stand, finding a glass of water and a couple of pills.

I love you, Helena.

When I turned back over, I noticed Damien sitting there, his feet on the bed while wearing the same clothes as the night before. His eyes were heavy from exhaustion, probably because he'd been up all night making sure I would last until morning. "You look like shit."

"Trust me, you don't look much better." I sat up then stripped off my leather jacket. I vaguely remembered being warm last night, kicking my feet to get the sheets as far away as possible. I rested my elbows on my knees and rubbed my face with my palms, still feeling sick even though I'd had nine hours to detox.

"I look better than you—any day." He lowered his feet from the bed and straightened. "Now, we're gonna talk about the shitshow last night. What happened?"

"I drank too much."

He gave me a cold look. "You let your guard down out in the open. What if someone spotted you and decided to take you out? What if you crossed paths with Maddox?"

"He'd be stupid to show his face in my city."

"Hades, come on. What happened with Sofia? You've broken up before and never lost your shit like this. What the hell happened?"

Destiny happened. "I asked her to marry me. She said no." That was the simplest explanation I could give. I put my heart out there, living in the moment, and it all went to shit. I wanted her in my house every night, safe under my roof. I wanted to fuck her every night in my bed. I wanted to help her run her hotel so she could have everything she wanted.

Damien gave me the most perplexed look I'd ever seen. "What the fuck were you thinking?"

I shrugged.

"You've known this girl for like two months."

I shrugged again. "It felt right."

"Felt right?" he asked incredulously. "Then ask her to move in with you. Tell her you love her. Start off small. I don't blame her for being freaked out."

If I'd asked her for any of those things, her reaction would have been the same. "That's not what bothers me the most."

"I figured there had to be something else for you to freak out like that. I almost drove you to the hospital. Your blood-alcohol level must still be high right now. It takes a lot for a grown man to be wasted. But with you...it takes a lot more than that. So I'm surprised you're alive right now."

A part of me wished I weren't. "She said she would never love me."

He sighed. "That's rough..."

She didn't say she didn't love me. She said she never would...as in, there was no chance of that happening. "It makes me wonder if the gypsy was right...she said I would love a woman, and she would never love me back."

"Hades, come on. You know that's bullshit."

"Is it?" I asked. "Because I've never felt anything like this before in my life. I've never given a damn about anyone besides the two of us. Then Sofia comes along...and I lose my mind. I can have any woman I could possibly want... except her. You think that's just a coincidence?"

"I think you're upset right now, so you're jumping to ridiculous conclusions." Damien was usually the impulsive one, and it was my job to calm him down. But perhaps seeing me lose my mind made him the calmer one. "There's no way that's true. I'll prove it. Did the gypsy say anything else about your future?"

"Yeah...that I would marry the woman."

"Really?" he asked. "Well, there you go. You aren't married, so it's bullshit."

"She said the woman still wouldn't love me even if we were married. She would give me two sons but still wouldn't love me. So it sounds like this will happen sometime in the future..."

Damien shook his head slightly. "That's never going to happen. I promise you. It's shitty that this happened to you, but it's her loss. You'll find someone else who won't play games."

That was the problem...I didn't want anyone else. I wanted to fuck beautiful women and get back to my life, but actually feeling something for someone...that was never going to happen. Whether that gypsy was full of shit or not, that was something she was right about.

I would never love another woman.

"I know what will cheer you up. I got tickets to the Barsetti Lingerie show. Conway Barsetti said he would take us backstage to meet the girls." He waggled his eyebrows. "What do you say? How about we get back on the horse?"

I had nothing else to do, and I wasn't keeping my dick in my pants. Sofia wasn't coming back, and even if she did, I wouldn't take her back. She humiliated me. I'd warned her not to cross me again, but she did it anyway.

It was over...and I wouldn't waste another second on her.

20

SOFIA

IT WAS A LONELY WEEK.

There were so many times I thought about calling...but what good would that do? The man asked me to marry him, and I said no. Not only did I break his heart, but I wounded his pride. Even if I changed my mind, I knew he wouldn't take me back.

Not that I had.

He hated me...and I hated him a bit too.

I hated him for ruining what we had. Everything was perfect, easy. He was the first man I'd ever met that I wanted so much. He was the best lover I'd ever had. No other man could replace what I'd just lost. I knew it wouldn't last forever, but by the time it ended, we would be sick of each other.

Now it had turned into a bitter breakup.

He hated me...I knew he did.

Why didn't he listen to me? Why didn't he do what I asked? Why did he have to destroy us?

Why?

I cradled the bottle of wine on the couch and kept drinking...because I had nothing else to do.

I SHOWED up at Gustavo's office the next morning.

"Surprised to see you here. Everything alright?" He rose from his desk to give me a hug.

"I was wondering if I could have my old job back." After careful consideration, I realized that my fantasies about the future were all bullshit. If I wanted this hotel, I had to fight for it. Once it was mine, I could make all the changes I wanted. I could cut ties to the criminals that used this place as a meeting location. I could divorce the man my mother forced me to marry once everything was mine.

I wanted this too much to give up.

Gustavo considered my request. "I thought you wanted to go in a different direction."

"Well, I changed my mind. One day, this hotel will be mine...and I'm willing to do anything to make that happen."

Gustavo had a much weaker resistance than my own mother, so he couldn't say no even if he wanted to. "Alright. It can't hurt to let you learn...especially now that you know the truth." He grabbed a pile of paperwork off his desk. "I want you to cook these books. We'll go over it later."

"Cook the books?" I asked, perplexed.

"Change the numbers to fit our real revenue."

Basically, hide all the blood money. "Got it..." I carried everything and headed into the hallway.

I had the worst luck in the world, so I ran into Hades, practically bumped into his chest and dropped all the documents in the process.

The look he gave me was terrifying. With wide-open eyes, he looked down into my face with the gaze of a killer. It was the same expression he'd given Lance in the alleyway, like he wanted to grab my throat and choke me to death. His shoulders stiffened in his gray suit, and his jaw clenched like he couldn't digest just how livid he was. There was so much hatred boiling in his blood that he couldn't handle it.

I froze in place, paralyzed by the spiteful energy coming from his body. He used to slide his hand into my hair and kiss me like I was the only thing that mattered to him. That stark contrast made this interaction even worse. Now I was witnessing the version his enemies experienced, the man everyone feared.

He was scary.

He didn't bend down and help me with the papers I'd scattered across the floor. His brown eyes were dark with rage as he stepped around me, disgusted with my presence.

"We're going to see each other often, so we should—"

"Don't speak to me. Ever." He moved closer to me, threatening me with his immense frame. He promised he would never hurt me, but he didn't need to touch me to accomplish that. This potent rage was damaging enough. After holding my gaze for another second, he walked past me and entered Gustavo's office.

I was left alone in the hallway, standing in a pile of papers... and my own isolation.

I WAS STILL SHAKEN up about my interaction with Hades.

He was a scary man.

But I reminded myself that this was his doing. He'd put me in a position I didn't want to be in, forced me into a corner with no escape. If I were the man and he were the woman, I never would have asked him to marry me. When a man didn't want commitment, no one batted an eye over it.

But Hades ignored everything I said, as if he got to decide what I wanted.

I stood alone in the lobby because the other receptionist was taking her lunch. That left me to think about Hades...to think about my life. Now, I wished I'd never met him, wished we'd never had that kiss on the balcony. Getting involved with him was my biggest regret. I'd have to see him for work on a regular basis...and it would always be a painful interaction.

Maybe in time, things would get better, but I suspected they would get worse. I'd grown frustrated by his coldness, so I would turn resentful. I'd mirror his rage, fueling the fire of his own anger. The situation would escalate, the fire would rise.

And we would hate each other more.

When he tried to push me for something more, I should have walked away...and stayed away. It was everything I hated about relationships, when a man tried to control a woman. Hades never respected my wishes, and he pushed for his own agenda. It was controlling and inappropriate.

Why would I want to marry someone like that?

Let alone a fucking drug dealer.

Asshole.

One of the Barsetti models stepped into the lobby, gliding across the floor in her five-inch heels. She wore a dress with a slit high up her thigh, skintight and perfect on her lovely curves. She had shoulder-length brown hair, styled in light curls. A black clutch was in her hand. She smiled as she looked out the main double doors.

Hades stepped inside a second later, his hands in his pockets. He was dressed casually, dark jeans and a long-sleeved black shirt. His jaw was cleanly shaven, and he looked at her with an appreciative gaze, his eyes taking in the sight of her lovely figure.

She moved into him anxiously, wrapping her arms around his neck and kissing him right in the lobby. Hades tensed like he hadn't been expecting that level of affection. She cupped his face and kissed him like she'd already fallen madly in love with him, like she understood how lucky she was to spend the evening with him.

I felt sick.

He had to pull away first because she wanted to keep kissing him.

It was like a car wreck. I couldn't stop staring.

He hooked his arm around her waist and escorted her outside with him, opening the door for her and taking her out to his car. He didn't give any indication that he knew I was standing at the counter. He could figure out when I was working when he wanted to, but maybe tonight he didn't check. Maybe he didn't care.

He put her in the black car that he'd driven me around in, the one where he'd held my hand as he drove me to his place. He started the car, the lights brightened, and he sped away, revving his powerful engine like he was showing off his new toy.

Then they were gone.

I hadn't moved since the horror show started to play out. I wasn't even sure if I'd taken a breath that entire time. It was just so sickening to look at, so damaging to my lungs, heart, and stomach.

I couldn't understand my feelings, couldn't understand the pain my blood was still trying to dissolve. Was I jealous? Was I hurt? Or did I just hate him? I said I didn't want to marry him, and I stood by that decision. Now I was even more grateful I'd said no. Why would I want to marry an asshole like that? Someone who tried to hurt me by showing off the model he'd be fucking tonight.

I detested relationships more than I ever had.

The good ones ended like this...and the bad ones never ended.

21

SOFIA

TWO YEARS LATER

IT ALL HAPPENED SUDDENLY.

Gustavo collapsed during dinner. The medics took him to the hospital. But he was dead before the doctor could even see him. The heart attack claimed his life two minutes after he gripped his chest and fell over.

Mother and I stood together at his gravesite. The coffin was lowered into the ground, and the priest said the final words of the service. Gustavo had an older son who was there with his family. He didn't shed a single tear, but there was so much emotion written across his face.

My mother didn't cry...at least, not in front of me.

I'd cried a lot over the past week. The man was my stepfather, but he was a good man. He took care of my mother and loved me like a daughter. He had this innate kindness that spread to every person around him. Even if he had criminal tendencies, he was still a good person.

I was going to miss him.

I wiped away a few tears, hot in my black dress in the summer sun.

The service ended, and people started to dissipate. The reception would be held in the ballroom of the hotel, the most fitting place to remember this man.

My arm moved to my mother's shoulder. "Would you like to stay a bit longer?"

"No." She stared at his coffin for a few more seconds before she turned away. "I've said goodbye."

As we walked across the grass away from the gravesite, Hades appeared on our left. In a black suit and tie, he approached us, tall and fit as he'd always been. His eyes never moved to me as he walked up to my mother and extended his hand. "I'm sorry for your loss, Maria." He took her hand and kissed her on the cheek.

"Thank you," she whispered. She was in a black dress with a black veil over part of her face. A black hat was on her head, protecting her scalp from the piercing rays of the sun. Her skin was pale like she didn't have enough blood in her veins. She was thinner too, like she hadn't taken a single bite since Gustavo died.

Hades ignored me—as always. The last time we spoke was years ago, when he told me never to speak to him again. His hostility never waned, and the longer it continued, the more I despised him.

The intensity had escalated until we couldn't even be in the same room together. We avoided each other like two magnets that had to be kept separated at all costs. If we came too close together, we'd collide in a harsh battle.

I expected him to be over it by now...but he wouldn't let it go.

Even though it'd been two fucking years.

Asshole.

He continued to look at my mother. "He was a good man."

"I know he was," she whispered. "We miss him so much."

Hades nodded. "I'm here if you need anything." He turned around and walked off.

It was my stepfather's funeral, and he couldn't put aside his differences to say a damn word to me, to extend any sympathy whatsoever. What I did to him was so terrible that he didn't think I even deserved that.

Biggest asshole on the planet.

I LEFT my apartment and moved back in with my mother.

She hated to be alone, couldn't stand it. She never formally asked me to return to the house, but she made a lot of pointed comments like, "It doesn't make sense for a pretty girl to live all alone. Are you eating enough? Without a chef, how can you make sure you're getting what you need?" I knew she didn't mean any of them. She was just too proud to ask me to come back home.

So I made the sacrifice.

It'd been a month since Gustavo had passed away, and she was quiet most of the time. We had breakfast together on the balcony every morning, talking about the hotel and other nonsense.

Now that Gustavo was gone, I was in charge. I'd learned so much in the past two years that I knew how to keep things flowing smoothly. Maybe my mother would realize that and let it be...but I suspected she wouldn't. I could tell people were treating me differently—and not in a good way. The board kept asking Hades for direction, and when Hades came by my office, he always communicated with the HR girl to get what he needed.

Cutting me out altogether.

I sat on the terrace with my mother that evening, dining on gnocchi in alfredo sauce while splitting a bottle of white wine. It was a warm day, but not nearly as humid as it'd been for the last couple weeks.

She'd started to eat again, to get back her faded vitality. "I don't want to get remarried." She made the statement with a sigh, like I'd provoked her with a question. "Gustavo wasn't supposed to die so young."

"Yeah...it's terrible." I was patient with my mother as she processed her loss. When she said rude things to me, I let them slide. She and I had our differences, but I loved her and I was there for her. But if I became a mother someday, I'd make sure to be nothing like her.

"I'm too old to start over again. Too old to find a husband."

"You aren't that old, Mother. But no, you don't need to get married again. It's fine to be on your own." There was no reason to be scared of independence. Once she had a bit of it, she'd probably enjoy it.

"I'm glad you feel that way. I've paid my dues..."

That was a sick attitude to have about it. That it was a sacrifice, an involuntary duty.

She set down her fork and folded her hands under her chin, giving me a pointed stare like she was about to say something. "We can't survive like this much longer. I've married two men I didn't love for this family. I've made enough sacrifices that I'm exonerated from further responsibility. Now it's your turn."

"My turn to what?"

"Marry."

My fork was stabbed into a gnocchi, but I didn't bring it to my lips. My fingers gripped the metal with frozen stillness.

"We need a powerful man to protect us. At my age, I won't be able to attract anyone of substance. I was lucky I found Gustavo after your father passed away. I won't get so lucky a third time. But you...you could have any man you want."

Why had I expected my mother to drop this? "I'm not marrying. I refuse."

"You refuse?" she asked, her voice cold and calculating. "How long do you think it'll be before the mafia runs us out of our own hotel? How long will it be before a powerful man squeezes us out and steals the ground beneath our feet?"

"If you're so worried about that, you shouldn't have done business with killers."

"That was your father's decision, not mine. Arguing about the past won't change our present. We both need you to do this to survive." She dropped her hands and maintained her cold stare. "There's no other way."

"I've been running the hotel just fine."

"That's not what I heard."

"From whom?" I snapped.

"The board doesn't respect you. And it won't be long until the men walk all over you. You're nothing but a pretty girl with a large inheritance. You're so inconsequential that people don't find you the least bit intimidating. I'm not saying this to hurt your feelings. I just want you to understand the situation."

I let the fork fall onto my plate with a clatter. "You're being ridiculous."

"No, I'm not. I've lost two husbands, and I don't want to lose my daughter too."

"Then let's sell the hotels. I'd rather lose my inheritance than be forced into marriage."

"And then what?" she asked. "You think we'll be safe? We're still accomplices of the men who use our hotel. If their enemies see us as easy targets, they'll punish us for sport. And I know you—you won't walk away from the business. So, either you marry...or we run."

I shook my head. "You've got to be kidding me."

"I wish I were."

"How can you expect me to just marry some random guy?"

"I did it twice. It's not so bad."

"Being beaten isn't so bad?" I asked incredulously.

"It wasn't always bad. There were a lot of good times. And most of all...I had you. You're the light of my life, Sofia. I know I don't say it enough, but you're everything to me. Never did I imagine I would have the most beautiful daughter in the world."

It was hard to stay mad at her when she said something so sweet.

"I know this isn't what you want. I know you deserve better. But this is the world we live in. You need to marry the right man to ensure a long and prosperous future for us. You can run the business under his protection, and no one will ever touch you. No one will touch me. And you can live a long and happy life."

"How can I be happy if I'm married to a man I don't love?"

"Maybe you'll love him someday. I did love both of my husbands...just not in a romantic way. We became friends, allies. We became partners. That companionship is much better than a combustive and lustful relationship that runs off emotion rather than logic. I think you'll like it more than you realize. And the two of you can always have your own arrangement. Make your relationship what you want it to be. Your father had his mistresses, and I was perfectly okay with it."

That was gross.

"Gustavo didn't. He didn't have the same kind of sexual appetite...because all men are different."

I didn't want to fall in love and get married anyway, so this seemed like a decent alternative. But I also didn't want to be the property of someone else, to be ordered around like a slave rather than a person.

"Sofia...you need to do this."

I sighed quietly.

"Please."

I wanted to run our family business more than anything, and I understood my mother's unease about the lack of protection. I saw the way men dismissed me like I was stupid, and I could also envision the bad men who came to our hotel being difficult. One night, they waltzed into the hotel and took over the bar like they owned the place. What would they have done if I'd stood up to them?

They would have killed me.

"I don't even know how we would do this. I mean, would we just send out a memo to rich dudes and tell them I'm looking for a husband? What would they get out of that?"

"For one, rich men all the want the same thing—a trophy wife. They want a beautiful woman who will give them beautiful children. You're are stunning, Sofia. Even by model standards, you're flawless."

"Well...thanks."

"Second, you don't need to worry about finding a husband. I already have someone in mind."

This just became real. "I won't marry someone if they're over ten years older than me. I'm not doing it."

"He's not. And he's very handsome too."

"Who is it?"

She smiled before she spoke, as if I would like the person she'd picked out. "Hades Lombardi."

I almost laughed because she couldn't possibly pick a worse guy. Yes, he was young, handsome, and rich, but he'd rather see me dead in a ditch than marry me. There was no one in the world who hated me more than him. "You'll have to find someone else."

"What's wrong with him?"

"He and I don't get along." I'd never told my mother about my relationship with him. If she knew he'd proposed to me and I said no, she would flip out.

"Really?"

"Yeah. There's no way in hell he'd be interested. And I'm not interested in him either."

"That's strange." She propped her chin on her fist as she looked at me. "Because when I spoke to him, he was extremely enthused."

My blood turned ice-cold. "What...?"

"Yes. In fact, he told me not to ask anyone else. He's in."

This was bad...very bad. "I'm not marrying him."

"Why not? He's got everything, Sofia. He's been smitten with you for years. I've seen the way he looks at you."

"He's an asshole."

"Really?" she asked. "I don't think an asshole would fight for you so hard."

"He doesn't like me. He just wants to marry me to torture me."

"I highly doubt that," she said. "He seemed genuine."

This couldn't be happening.

"Hades is, by far, the best match. He's young, extremely powerful, handsome, and he's got resources we can't even dream of. No one will touch you as his wife. No one will dare cross you. You can run that hotel however you want. You'll get everything you want."

"No."

"Sofia—"

"I said no." I didn't turn him down just so I could marry him years later.

"Well, I've already agreed to it."

"Then you marry him," I snapped. "I'm not going to do it."

She tilted her head slightly as she watched me. "Talk to him first before you make a decision."

"I have nothing to say to him."

"But maybe he has something to say to you."

22

HADES

MY ASSISTANT SPOKE TO ME OVER THE INTERCOM. "I KNOW you're busy, sir. But Maria Romano is here to see you. She says it's important."

I stared at the phone as I sat behind my desk, considering the request. Gustavo had been gone for a month, and she probably needed help with the hotel. I was doing my part behind the scenes, making sure people stayed in line and didn't take advantage of Sofia.

She was such an easy target. "I'll see her."

Maria stepped inside, dressed in a Chanel blazer with a gold bracelet on her arm. Her wedding ring was still on her left hand. With her hair pinned back eloquently and gold earrings hanging from her lobes, she was a classy woman with timeless looks.

Sofia had inherited everything from her.

I rose to my feet and greeted her with a kiss on the cheek. "How are you, Maria?"

"I've been better, of course." She smoothed out her skirt then sat down, crossing her long legs and showing off her prominent heels that she had no problem pulling off. Her hands came into her lap, and she stared at me, sighing as she smiled. "And you?"

"I'm well." My life was the same bullshit every day. I processed blood money, kept it safe from the wrong people, and continued my drug operation in plain sight. Maddox and I were still at war with each other, taking shots but always missing. Various women graced my bed, but of course, they never meant a thing to me.

Not that Sofia did either.

"How can I help you?" I'd enjoyed working with Gustavo, so I extended the same respect to his widow. She was vulnerable without him, owning a business she couldn't control much longer.

"This might sound a bit startling...but I've noticed the way you look at my daughter."

I went rigid in my chair because I hadn't anticipated a statement like that. I could read people well, predict what would happen next. But she dropped that bomb on me without warning.

"I've noticed it for years. Sofia is a jewel. She's so beautiful and so damn smart. I just wish she would keep that attitude in check."

I had no idea where this was going.

"Anyway, with Gustavo gone, I fear for our safety and our livelihood. I'm too old to take another husband, and Sofia needs to start her family in the next few years anyway. So... I'm looking for potential suitors."

"Does she know this?"

"Not yet. I wanted to compile a list of men before I approached her about it."

She was asking me to marry her daughter. Sofia obviously had never told her about our relationship, not even after we broke up. "Have you asked anyone else?"

"No. You're my first pick. So...is that something you're interested in?"

Over the last few years, I'd tried to convince myself that my fortune was untrue. It was just a coincidence. It didn't mean anything. But now the opportunity to marry Sofia had fallen into my lap, and if I said yes, it would become reality.

Goose bumps burst across my arms.

Maria shifted her gaze back and forth to gauge my thoughts.

If I married Sofia, she would never love me. I would be in the same situation as before...infatuated with a woman who didn't give a damn about me. It would be a stupid idea to go down that road again, to settle for less than what I deserved. I had too much self-respect to go through that bullshit... especially when I knew it would never be real.

But if I said no...she would marry someone else.

Someone else would fuck her every night.

Someone else would be a father to her children.

Someone else would get to enjoy her every day until they died.

This woman would never love me...but at least I got to love her.

It was better than nothing. "Yes...I'm interested."

She smiled. "Perfect. I have a few more men on the list—"

"No." I didn't mean to be rude and cut her off, but I wasn't bringing anyone else into the mix. If another man were given the opportunity, he would fight until she was his. It would turn into a bloody war. "I'm marrying her."

Maria's smile slowly faded away. "I guess I was right about you. You've always wanted my daughter."

"Yes."

"I have a couple conditions, Hades."

"Alright." I would agree to whatever she wanted.

"I know you're a rich man who doesn't need money, but I'll give you half of the hotel as a thank-you for protecting my daughter. If it ends in divorce, it's still yours. But I ask that you never leave her, that you promise to stay committed to her and do whatever it takes to stay together. That you make sure she never leaves."

That was an easy promise to make. "Alright."

"I love my daughter very much. I want to know that you'll take care of her...that you'll never hurt her. My first husband beat me on a regular basis. I never want her to experience the same thing."

It was touching that she'd asked at all. "I'm not that kind of man. I kill those kinds of men. Nothing will ever happen to your daughter, I promise. I'd die before I let anything happen to her."

"Good answer." She rose to her feet. "I'll talk to her about this. It'll take some time to get her to agree, but I'll make it happen."

I rose to my feet and walked her to the door.

"I have to ask," she said. "You're only thirty-one and so handsome. Why would you agree to marry?"

I couldn't tell her the truth, that I was still in love with her daughter years later. I masked my feelings with hatred and bitterness, but once you really loved someone...you never stopped. "She's the most beautiful woman I've ever seen. I'd have to be stupid not to want her."

ALSO BY PENELOPE SKY

Two years of bitter loneliness have passed. The woman I love is now the woman I hate. I lose myself in beautiful women every night and tell myself that fortune reading was nothing but a scam.

But then her mother asks me to marry her.

I say yes.

Now this woman will be mine forever.

Maybe the prophecy really is true. I'm committing to a woman that will never love me in return.

But it was better to be her husband than allow someone else to take my place. It was better to conquer her body every night than be lonely with someone else.

Much better.

Order Now

Made in the USA
Columbia, SC
23 September 2019